to Touch and to be Touched

AF520659

notionpress.com

to Touch and to be Touched

Chinmayee Tripathy

notionpress
.com

Notion Press

Old No. 38, New No. 6

McNichols Road, Chetpet

Chennai - 600 031

First Published by Notion Press 2015

ISBN 978-93-5206-598-1

To

Two very special people:

My wonderful, affectionate and compassionate companion Pavi, who is my heart,

and

my sweet and lovely daughter, Tabli, who is my life.

"My heart and my soul, together, make me whole"

With Love,
Linu/Mamma

CHAPTER ONE

Edison, New Jersey; August 2014

Opening her eyes and stretching her hand to the right side of her bed, Anurati searched for Ardhendu in the middle of the night. "Where is he?" she thought and turned towards the washroom. No light was seen from under the washroom door. Pushing down her comforter halfway through her body and leaning her upper half against the bed's headboard, she tried to catch hold of her sleepy head and her not-so-long black silky hair pulling them into a knot. Gasping for breath, she got up and covered herself with a maroon silk robe, which concealed her sexy unending legs and slim fair hands.

"Oh! Dear, you are making me so exhausted at just three months! I just cannot imagine the rest of my *balloon-body*!" said Anurati, covering the lower part of her abdomen with both her palms. Anurati went to the balcony of her bedroom and slid the glass door open, expecting to see Ardhendu over there.

"Huh! Where has he gone, and that too in the middle of the night?" murmured Anurati. She slowly walked down the stairs towards her living room, looking left and right. On the left, she saw a bottle of water with its cap open in the kitchen with the chimney light on. She immediately guessed that Ardhendu had helped himself to a hot cup of tea. She moved towards the sink to check for the empty cup, but it wasn't there. She switched on the kitchen light and turned off the chimney light. Yawning, Anurati took a large mouthful of oxygen. She closed the water bottle and started moving towards the living area. "He must have dug himself into the extra spongy couch, let me check," murmured Anurati. She found the large leather couch empty. She could sense that Ardhendu, her loving husband, was missing and nowhere to be seen. She began taking deep breaths and sat on the couch.

"Don't worry Anu. Relax. Calm down," Anurati tried consoling herself. She poured herself a glass of water from the jug on the coffee table and drank it in a gulp. This was all because of her pregnancy. She was exhausted and felt like she couldn't even walk around in her duplex condo. Her obstetrician had told her to keep herself hydrated throughout her pregnancy. After relaxing for a few minutes, she pounced onto the cordless right next to where she was sitting, as if something charged inside her. She dialled Ardhendu's mobile number at top speed. Earlier, we used to remember all our friends' and relatives' phone numbers, but now that job is properly and efficiently done by the mobile device. Search for the name. The phone dials the number for you. However, the numbers that are close to our heart stay imprinted in our memory. Yes, Anurati was madly in love with Ardhendu Mishra – her husband, her guide, her godfather, her *WORLD*.

Sitting in front of a lake, Ardhendu was searching for ways to let Anurati know what he had heard just half-an-hour ago. Terrified after hearing the news, he silently slipped out of the house without making any noise, without disturbing his wife and unborn baby. He had driven to the park nearby to get some peace of mind rather than making pieces of his mind. Anurati's parents had both died three years ago from cardiac arrests in their sleep. They were peaceful deaths, happening just four days apart. The news of their death was a shock to Anurati. It happened right after her marriage to him. However, with time, she had grown stronger and even matured to understand the cycle of life. Now in her thirties, she understood life better and was going to enter into motherhood. Ardhendu wondered, "How am I going to drop this *bomb on* her? I can't! I shouldn't!" Ardhendu started walking towards the lake. He saw his reflection in the water. He felt like he had no courage to face Anurati. All of a sudden, he was grabbed by two policemen from behind.

"Don't move! It's the Police," said one.

"What are you up to?" questioned the other.

"Hold on! Hold on, please! Don't handcuff me. I am Ardhendu Mishra from India. I am a software engineer and hold a valid New Jersey driver's licence in my car. I have a valid passport. Whatever you want, let's talk about it. Please undo the cuffs. Please, don't shoot!" Ardhendu shouted frantically, without missing a breath. Folding his hands behind him, locking the cuffs, the policeman turned Ardhendu around to face him. Looking at him, they both put their guns back into the holster.

"Trying to commit suicide, young man?" asked one of the officers.

"Believe me, I was…"

The other officer cut in, "But you look too worn out and depressed! It's 3:00 AM!"

"Yes, officer, I got some tragic news from my country and my wife is pregnant. I just can't decide what I should do. Should I hide it from her? Or should I tell her? I am scared. If she takes it badly, and if I lose my unborn child…. If…" Ardhendu choked between his words and tears rolled down from his eyes. Fighting for words and kneeling down, digging his face into the grass, hands still in the cuffs, he said, "My wife lost her *last and only* family, her younger brother, in a road accident in Bangalore early this morning!"

One of the policemen caught Ardhendu by his shoulder, made him stand up and started dragging him towards the only car that was parked nearby.

"That's your car?" asked the officer.

"Yes, yes!" replied Ardhendu breathlessly.

After walking some fifty meters, the other policeman unlocked the latch of the handcuffs, and ordered him to show him his documents. Sweat rolled down Ardhendu's temple to his masculine greenish fair-complexioned cheek. He wiped it immediately and took out his car keys from the pocket of his trousers hurriedly. He was out in his pyjamas, which made no difference to him. Ardhendu opened his car doors and saw his mobile phone ringing, flashing Anurati's beautiful picture, as if blowing him a kiss. He was about to answer the call but was stopped by the cops. Soon, one of them snatched it from his hands, started gazing at the display picture, and read the name out loud. "*SWEETU.*"

"Okay, young man! Your wife?" asked the policeman, nosily.

"Yes, officer," answered Ardhendu taking out his driver's licence from his purse which he remembered he threw along with his house keys onto the front seat.

"So Mr Mishra, it wasn't a pleasant meeting but we are sorry to cause you trouble. We are on duty," said one of the policemen, thoroughly scrutinizing his driver's licence. Immediately, the other officer slid back his gun into his holster and apologized to Ardhendu and asked to convey condolences to his lovely lady and told him to take care of her, as destiny has its way for a smooth ride in life. Shaking hands with each other, they drove away the white and blue car with the coloured lights shining and the beacon flashing in the dark. Soon, his phone stopped ringing. Holding his mobile in both his hands, which were now shaking, Ardhendu sat in the car seat and was thinking about his encounter with police. He was scared. Taking deep breaths, he said, "All is well that ends well." His phone rang again – and it was Anurati calling. He disconnected the call again. This was the second call from Anurati. Ardhendu felt lucky that he need not have to answer much and dialled back.

"Hello!" Anurati answered the call from the other side.

"Sweetu, is everything fine with you? Are you alright?" asked Ardhendu in almost one breath, sounded genuinely worried for her.

"What?" Anurati yelled. Without giving him a chance to speak, she said, "It is you who is missing from the house! Not answering the phone in the middle of the night… sorry… early in the morning!" clarified Anurati. "Where are you? How are you? Is everything alright?"

Ardhendu calmly listened to her and finally got a chance to speak. "Calm down, Anu. It's not good for our baby!"

"Okay! When will you be home?" Anurati asked, worried.

"In a few minutes, dear. I will explain it to you then. Bye for now," said Ardhendu, disconnecting the call.

For two minutes, Ardhendu closed his eyes, and sat, relaxing in his car, thinking of all that had happened. First, the call from India. Then, his encounter with the police. And now, the ordeal was still not over. He had to convey the sad news to his pregnant wife.

In a hurry, Ardhendu browsed through his contacts and started searching amongst those listed under D. He found the name he was looking for. Tapping the name in the phone, which he had kept in speaker mode, he waited as the phone rang and went to an IVR tone asking for a message. Ardhendu recorded his message after the beep. "Hello, Doctor, this is Ardhendu Mishra, your patient Anurati's husband. I want to meet you in the clinic tomorrow morning. Please confirm." Disconnecting the call, Ardhendu started the car. Now with the moving wheels his thoughts too started to roll." Oh my god! What have I done? I dialled the doctor's clinic and without even bothering, I left a voice message. What if the doctor gets back to Anurati and asks for the reason for the emergency visit?" Talking aloud to himself, he applied sudden brakes to his moving vehicle and he stopped with a huge jerk. Luckily, he was driving recklessly when there was no traffic at all. He was the only one to drive at those wee hours.

"Now what?" Thinking hard, he decided, "What is done is done. I cannot change anything now. I should go home to Anurati first and think of a better plan after discussing with the doctor, if all goes well till that time."

Ardhendu consoled himself and drove fast. In no time, he reached the parking lot where he parked his car and went inside. By the time he reached home, Anurati was relaxing in the brown leather couch, fast asleep. Ardhendu went to Anurati. Cupping her jaws, he kissed her on her forehead. Immediately, Anurati opened her eyes and struggled to get up from her sleep posture. She was actually not that heavy the way she used to treat herself but she was extra protective about herself for her first pregnancy. Her doctor had given some guidelines to get up, which she followed religiously. Now that she was struggling to get up, Ardhendu gave her a helping hand, put a pillow behind her back and made her comfortable.

"Where were you?" asked Anurati.

"Anu, I just went to the lake side to get some fresh air," Ardhendu answered gently.

"Liar," Anurati said a bit loudly. She turned her head away from Ardhendu.

"Listen to me, I went to our bedroom patio and thought of driving to the lake, like we always do, but things are not same as it used to be few months' back. You need more rest. So I didn't want to disturb you and went alone instead," said Ardhendu.

"But now I..." she said, but Ardhendu interrupted. "You won't believe it! I was handcuffed by NJ cops half-an-hour ago," said Ardhendu restlessly.

"What?" Anurati was shocked at what she heard. Her mouth was wide open and she stared blankly at Ardhendu. "Then?"

"Then what? Nothing! I saw my reflection in the lake. They misunderstood it, thinking I was trying to commit suicide!" giggled Ardhendu.

But deep inside, he was hiding the truth, his genuine fear and his tears from the tragic news of the sad demise of Aniket, Anurati's younger brother. His primary concern was to keep Anurati happy and smiling without any stress. Without much exaggeration, he poured himself a glass of water and quenched his thirst.

"Then?" Anurati asked curiously. "Please, this time, explain things. Were you scared?" She was irritated.

"I showed them my documents and they released me, apologizing for what they did to a respectable person," Ardhendu stressed on the last two words. Without letting Anurati speak, he said, "Now I am standing in front of you with a glass of water in hand!" He sipped the water after making a gracious toast.

It was still dark outside. Both of them went upstairs hand-in-hand. Ardhendu helped Anurati and tucked her in. She seemed relaxed with Ardhendu back, lying on her side under the same comforter. But deep inside, she was very disturbed at the thought. "Ardhendu has started with signs of his phobia again! Did he really attempt suicidal? Was he caught by the cops for that? Is he telling the truth? Do I need to contact Dr. Saxena? Or should I wait for something serious to happen?"

Soon, she closed her eyes and fell into a deep sleep. It was Ardhendu who sat up, restless, with numerous thoughts in his mind, making him feel as if he was in a giant wheel, falling down after making a full circle from high above. He was literally visualizing his fearful thoughts: *The phone call... the accident... the death... the cops... the hard grip of the handcuff on his wrists...a fearful, tensed Anu.* But again, all these could not stop Ardhendu from falling asleep, as his tired body went inside the cosy warm comforter with his sexy wife inside. He felt the soft touch of her breast against his back. He indulged himself in her loving cuddle, as she draped one leg over his hip and one hand around his tummy. Her sleepy breath brushed against the back of his neck, and its rhythmic pattern put him to sleep.

CHAPTER TWO

Rourkela, Odisha; November 1996

Anurati Acharya was the eldest daughter of her family, the Acharya Brahmins in the colony. Her father was a Government servant at the BSNL (Bharat Sanchar Nigam Limited) and her mother was a private school teacher. Her brother Aniket was a year younger to her, so he was just like a buddy. He was always prompted by their father to address Anurati as 'Anu Di', but he only said, "Chill Pops! She is like a friend," and winked at Anurati. Both Anurati and Aniket were in the same school. She was in Class VI and he was in Class V. Aniket had his eleventh birthday a few days ago and was super excited to get a *Hero-Ranger* bicycle from his father. For both kids, their father was a *super-dad.* Now that Aniket also had a bicycle, they rode down to school pedalling all the way from home instead of school bus. His birthday was a day before their *Diwali vacations* began. Anurati and Aniket pedalled all the way to school with their friends Ardhendu Mishra, Gourav Rout and Lisa Rout who were already waiting for them. Gourav was Aniket's friend and his sister Lisa was Anurati's. Mishra uncle's only son was Ardhendu, whose mother died after his delivery. Everyone was sympathetic towards Ardhendu and always said, "Unlucky, motherless child." But all these discussions were always done behind his back, which Anurati vehemently protested saying, "Why say such things when his father fulfils his every need and plays the role of both mother and father very nicely?"

Riding between the lanes without any traffic signals on the way, the kids were together and were safe on their bicycles. Parents never worried about accidents or mishaps. The drive was about ten minutes from their houses. Soon, they locked their cycles in the cycle stand and waved to each other before going to their respective classes. Lisa and Anurati walked hand-in-hand. Gourav and Aniket kicked little pebbles and started walking towards their classes, chatting about the previous day's game in the backyard. Ardhendu was quiet and alone. He waved to all of them and went to class. He was the senior-most amongst them and was in Class IX. Ardhendu was a bright student and was an example to the younger kids. He was a fair and handsome boy and was well-groomed. Now that he was in his early adulthood, adolescence had touched his face and had left him with a slightly swollen Adam's apple with a slightly hoarse voice. His fair skin showed slight signs of the greenish stubble of the beginnings of facial hair. His hair was perfectly trimmed. He had a nice haircut. The day went by quickly and the kids were excited for the upcoming festival and the vacations. As the classes got over, they waved to each other and wishing each other saying, 'Happy holidays!' All five pedalled back home. As they reached Lisa's house, she found her parents waiting for them to board the taxi. "Lisa, Gourav… Come on! Hurry up. There's very little time left for the train to leave!" shouted Jagan Rout, their father, at the top of his voice. The kids were dumbstruck. Both shouted in chorus, "Where are we going?"

"It's your *Nanu.* We got a telegram stating he is on his deathbed," said Mrs. Rout, sobbing. All their smiles were lost in a fraction of a second. Lisa and Gourav parked and locked their bicycles and went straight inside the taxi.

"Aunty, when will you all be back?" Anurati asked, shocked.

"I will let you know Anu, I will be staying at home," answered Rout Uncle gazing at her from top to bottom. His eyes moved slowly past her curves. Anurati was old enough to understand these nasty looks.

"Anu, take this and give it to your mamma," Mrs. Rout handed a folded paper to Anurati as if it was something confidential.

"Oh! Sure, Aunty. You take care," Anurati said as the taxi drove away.

"Anu, now what shall we do? What about our Diwali celebrations, bursting crackers? We will be bored, *yaar*," Aniket said, kicking a stone. "Aru *bhaiya*, you are staying at home, right?" Aniket asked Ardhendu doubtfully.

"Don't worry, Aniket. We shall have our share of fun together," Ardhendu said and waved at them before entering the garage of the next building. After some rounds of cycling, Anurati and Ardhendu were home, too. The three adjacent buildings were shared by five friends.

Leaving her shoes outside, Anurati went straight to her mother in the kitchen and gave her the note saying, "This is from Rout Aunty!" Without waiting for a response, she went straight to her bedroom. Earlier, both kids shared their rooms. Now that Anurati had grown up, she was given her privacy. Her private world was a 10 x10 room with a pinkish-white bed, maintained neatly without any creases. She had a pink extra-soft pillow with matching pillow covers, a big yellow teddy bear which was her birthday gift when she was four; a white desk with a rotating executive chair; and a very tall cupboard with transparent glass sliders and opaque aluminium doors – half of which was filled with books and other half with dresses. Now that she had sanitary pads under her dresses, she was instructed by her mother to keep them out of sight from Aniket. As soon as Anurati went inside her room, she locked it from inside. She took out her green pyjamas with a flowery top and changed her uniform. She gazed at herself in the mirror. She was no longer a little girl. She had developed small protrusions in her chest and was now wearing a properly-sized cover to protect them. She remembered the first day when her mother helped her with the hook of her bra and even explained to her about the biological clock that started just two months ago. She was terrified at the bleeding but was later relieved to know that she wasn't suffering from a disease but had stepped into the world of adulthood. She remembered that her mother had told her to keep this to herself – a secret. When her mother explained, Aniket was in the playground and her father was in the office. Only she and her mother discussed this together, and it made Anurati speechless. She was asked to remember the first date when she bled so that she could be well-prepared for the next cycle. Anurati circled the date in her calendar which was pasted on the back of her cupboard door. She was concerned after what happened the second time she had her menses. She had stained her school uniform which her mother noticed and scolded her, and told her not to repeat the mistake. Anurati was dressed properly, cleaned up her room, put her bags and uniform in their proper places. She was much more organized than her brother. "Ten more days to go," she murmured, checking the calendar before shutting the cupboard door. She went straight inside the washroom to freshen up.

Anurati's mother was a primary school teacher in the school nearby. By 1:00 PM, she returned home and prepared the meals and cleaned up the house. Anurati admired her mother. She came out of her room and went straight to the dining table where Aniket was already busy munching his snack. "Why the hurry, Aniket? Gourav is not here. Did you forget?" teased Anurati.

"Come on Anu, I am going to *Bhaiya's* place. He asked me to join him for video games." Without letting Anurati speak, Aniket asked her to join them for the games. Before Anurati could answer, her mother refused and asked him to go alone as she wanted Anurati's help on something. Anurati watched all this silently. The decision was made before she could get a word in edgewise. Aniket went out without wasting a second.

"What was the note from Aunty, mamma?"

"Rout Aunty had written she won't be back for fifteen days but your uncle will stay here. So I have to serve him breakfast and dinner. He will have lunch in his office canteen."

"What about lunch on Saturday and Sunday?"

"Shut up! Why will I feed on weekends? He can prepare his own food! Your Aunty had especially mentioned weekdays only!"

Anurati listened to what her mother explained but could not understand the depth of what her mother really meant. In the absence of a wife, taking care of a lonely husband is very critical. How much was asked was what one had to follow, or else, it might be a matter of gossip and the "good friend" image would be tarnished. Anurati's mother asked her to do whatever she felt like, and that she would deliver the meals when asked. Anurati left the table and was in her room with her walk-man. She was fond of Hindi songs. When she did nothing else, she put on her headphones on and relaxed, listening to old melodies and humming along. The last song always remained on her mind all day. She was alone, but was very happy with herself and thanked god for those silent golden moments.

"Anu, Anu, Anu…" shaking her head, her mother woke her up. Anurati didn't realize that she had slept for two long hours in the evening. She rubbed her eyes and stared at her mother blankly, and asked her what the matter was and why she woke her up so early. It was a long weekend, there was no school and there were no tuitions! She dug her head into her pillow, frowning at her mother. Her mother pulled her shoulder and made her sit up. Gently cupping her face, she said, "It is 9:00 PM! You have the whole night to sleep. Please just go and give Rout Uncle dinner and come fast, so that we can eat."

This loving kind gesture made Anurati lean against her mother's body. She hugged her tight and kissed her on her stomach and jumped out of bed. She asked about Aniket.

"Video games, you forgot?" replied Anurati's mother passing the box to her.

"Don't worry mamma I will bring him back," said Anurati and left for Rout Uncle.

"Hi, Anu," waved Aniket, entering the gate which Anurati opened for her to go out. Anurati shouted to him to slow down, but he was too excited to show her his stunts, so he raced inside the main gate and finally applied the brake and looked at Anurati. "See? Everything is under control!"

He parked his bicycle, praising himself. He came to Anurati. She insisted that Aniket deliver the food to Rout Uncle, but Aniket was tired enough and even didn't want to accompany her. He kissed his sister on her cheek, and praised her for doing such good work. She waved goodbye and went inside. Now Anurati had no choice and thought it was a waste of time if she approached her brother again to do this. She walked alone to Rout Uncle's house. On her way, she saw Ardhendu bicycling somewhere. She thought of calling him, but didn't. Soon, she reached Lisa's house, but didn't expect her friend at this time as she knew that only Rout Uncle was at home. She rang the doorbell and her uncle opened the door, busy on the phone.

He was holding his cordless, and was busy chatting and just nodded at Anurati. He made some signals for Anurati to go into the kitchen. Anurati could understand what he meant and went straight to the kitchen, unloaded the food into plastic containers and covered them for uncle. She then put the empty boxes back into the polythene cover, which she took back with her. She did everything fast and was lost in thought. She was unaware that uncle had already disconnected his call and was busy staring at her extremely perfect slim profile with all the curves in the right places. She looked ravishing and Rout Uncle, instead of staring from outside the kitchen door, came inside and stood just behind her, slightly touching her.

"Ouch! You scared me uncle!"

"I am sorry, Anu."

"It's okay, you called Aunty? When are they going to come back? What about our Diwali celebrations, uncle?" Anurati felt awkward at the silence. His closeness was weird, so she kept talking and moving away from him. She thought of covering the *Kheer,* the rice pudding, that she had just unloaded, but left it uncovered. She searched for her polythene cover, grabbed it and started moving out of the kitchen, out of the main door that was thankfully open. But to her surprise, uncle stopped her by holding her shoulders from behind. This touch frightened Anurati. Even her father had never caught hold of her like this! She didn't dare look back and she didn't stop. She kept walking hurriedly and was out of the main door. She was terrified. Once she was out of the house, she relaxed and found that she was breathing hard and her heartbeat was audible to her ears. She could not understand what he was up to. She only thought of those villains in movies who misbehaved with the heroines. Before she could think of anything else, uncle came out and stood exactly behind Anurati, cupping her tiny breasts in both his hands, as if unaware of who she was. He asked her shamelessly as to why she had just kept the food and was running away from him. So what if her friend Lisa was not there? He asked her to spend time with him so that they could chat together. Anurati could not believe what was happening to her and what this man was doing! "Leave me alone!" she shouted and forced her way out of his grasp. She ran away from him towards the main gate. She was unable to see ahead of her, with her eyes full of tears. She was unable to hear what uncle said. She was unable to understand what that man had done to her when she collided with Ardhendu, who was just outside the main gate.

"Watch out Anu!" shouted Ardhendu. Anurati was shedding tears and was literally frightened. She was shaking when Ardhendu held her tight and shook her, shouting her name loudly again and again. "Anu, Anu… Are you alright?"

"Uncle is so bad. I won't come here again, never."

Ardhendu was mature enough to understand what Anurati tried to say. He nodded and closed his fist, as if to punch something hard. He controlled himself, and consoling Anurati, he accompanied her till she reached her house safely, and waved goodbye. Anurati found no one in the living room. She went straight inside her room and locked herself inside. She wiped her tears which were flowing constantly and splashed water on her face. Every time she closed her eyes, uncle's touch was all she could feel. She kept splashing water on her face and finally, a knock on her door awakened her. She patted her face dry and opened the door. She found Aniket. Anurati thought of not disclosing this incident to anyone. What would she tell anyone if at all she tried explaining herself? Once, she thought she would tell her mother that uncle pulled her and tried pressing her. What? But again, she was confused and thought of not saying anything to anyone. She decided she wouldn't go to him again. She will try to avoid him all her life if she could help it. With all these thoughts in mind, she thought of Ardhendu. How cool was he! He consoled her, accompanied her and even made her comfortable without asking about the incident. What if he had asked what that monster had tried to do to her? She wouldn't have been able to answer him! Before Anurati's mother started with her interrogations, she simply said that she left the food covered in Rout Uncle's kitchen as he was busy on the phone. Anurati's heart desperately wanted to call that man a monster instead of saying uncle, but she had made up her mind not to disclose this to anyone. She remained calm and finished dinner. After dinner, her only work was to sleep. But after this incident she could not. She could visualize the touch, his act of cupping his palms, his grasp – and how tight and hard it was. It all scared her. Why did he do that? Anurati was too young to understand these things. She thought of Ardhendu. She thought she could share her feelings with him. She would also ask Ardhendu what he had guessed about the incident. She only said, "Uncle is bad," but he didn't even bother to ask her why, what but instead he consoled her. All these thoughts made her sleep. Anurati was physically touched by that *b*****d*! She was terrified. That middle-aged man didn't even have the fear of being caught for what he had done to the girl. He should have treated her as his own daughter, but what he did was really shameful! Ardhendu was shy by nature, but was not a fool. He was matured enough to understand what Rout Uncle was up to. He was a motherless child, so his father's deeds exposed him to certain truths of life. The evening's incident had shaken him as well. When Anurati shouted about uncle's touch, Ardhendu was passing by uncle's house. Listening to Anurati's scream, he had stopped his bicycle in front of the gate. He saw what uncle was doing to Anurati. He was scared. He went to the side and parked his bicycle. He tried gathering courage and moved inside the gate to rescue Anurati, when she collided with him with tears in her eyes. From her tears, he could sense that what uncle had done to her was wrong! He had seen his father doing such things with Aunty, who in return, kissed his father back, rather than running away from him. Ardhendu was not concerned about what his father was doing. Rather, he was concerned about Anurati. Was this mere attraction towards Anurati? Or was it love? Ardhendu tried closing his eyes but the memory of Anurati colliding with him was what he was most disturbed by. "Why am I not able to sleep? Tomorrow, I shall go to Rout Uncle and ask him what he was trying to do with Anurati!" After some time, he decided he wouldn't go, instead, he would meet Anurati first. By then, he took his mother's photo, which was beautifully framed in a silver frame. He held it close to his heart. Ardhendu closed his eyes and soon fell asleep.

CHAPTER THREE

Edison, New Jersey; August 2014

"Thank you doctor for giving me your precious time," Ardhendu thanked Anurati's obstetrician at her clinic.

"It's my duty," said the doctor and started enquiring about Anurati's condition and what made him book an appointment earlier than the scheduled one for Anurati's first trimester check-up. "Yes, doctor! I know her next appointment is next week," said Ardhendu. He explained the news of Aniket's road accident in Bangalore that he had hidden from Anurati. He told her how he was concerned about her getting into shock if she knew about her younger brother's sudden demise. He tried explaining how he had not yet disclosed the news and asked for her suggestions regarding this. "I am sorry to hear this, Mr Mishra," said the doctor and asked him how long he could keep this as a secret. Ardhendu honestly replied that it was very tough to keep this hidden from Anurati. But if she said he had to do this for Anurati's and the baby's sake, then he could do it for all his life.

"No, no, Mr Mishra, no need of doing this all your life," the doctor said clearly and suggested that he bring Anurati for a check-up as per schedule. After doing her routine check-up, she would tell him what would be best for both would-be mommy and the baby. "Hope this is fine with you Mr Mishra?"

"Of course doctor, see you next week then." The doctor prepared herself for the next patient while Ardhendu left.

"May I come in?" a voice outside the door made the doctor smile. A tall handsome man in his early fifties peeped inside the door by slightly opening the door. "Hope I didn't disturb you, madam," said the man teasing the doctor.

"Come on please, stop this. I am with my patient," said the doctor smiling back at him.

"Mr Ardhendu, you are here? How are you?"

"Yes Dr. Saxena, she is my wife's obstetrician. We are expecting a baby," Ardhendu pointed towards the doctor. Dr. Saxena congratulated Ardhendu and asked him to take care of himself and his wife. He asked him if he was still on his medication and therapies or if they were over. He was happy that he had overcome his fear and was leading a very normal life, unlike most other phobia patients who suffered lifelong. The other doctor interrupted asking how long they had known each other for, as by now she understood that Mr Mishra was her husband's patient. After a brief chat, Ardhendu left the room. Dr. Saxena, the psychiatrist, told his wife about Ardhendu's condition, of how he suffered from Haphephobia, the strangest phobia that can occur, the origin of which was predicted to be his background, his loneliness, his early exposure to unacceptable behaviour and even situations of trauma. Whatever was the cause, the bottom-line was that he once was haphephobic, and now, he seemed to have been cured.

"You know whom he was scared of the most?" He laughed out loud and said, "The love of his life."

"But they are a very nice couple. Nothing seems wrong between them and I must say your patient is a very caring and loving husband. Where did the baby come from, then?" she giggled and hugged her husband.

With Anurati's pregnancy and the happiness that it brought, Ardhendu had forgotten about his past. He was not on any medication anymore. He was not on any treatment any longer. He was healthy and fit. However, he suddenly realized that he was sweating heavily. He turned the car's air-conditioner to the coolest level. He wiped off the sweat that rolled from his temple and kept saying, "I am alright. I am fine!" These magical words helped him reach his parking spot in front of his condominium. Anurati saw Ardhendu's car and opened the door. She waited for him eagerly. But five minutes later, she saw no movement inside the car. She thought of shouting out to him, but the glass windows were shut so it was useless. She put on her slippers, adjusted her gown over her body and walked to the car. She saw Ardhendu sweating, his fists were holding the steering wheel rather tight. She saw him breathing heavily and murmuring something that wasn't audible. The car engine was still on. "Aru, Aru? Open the door! Roll down the window!" Anurati banged the window from outside, shouting his name repeatedly. She saw no movement from his side, only his lips uttering something.

"I am alright, I am fine," Ardhendu was still repeating these words. Ardhendu saw Anurati banging the glass pane and smiled at her. He opened the window and said, "I am alright. I am fine, Anu!" Yes, of course, you are fine! It is I who is pregnant, my dear husband!" Anurati tried lightening the atmosphere. He asked why she was outside and guessed she must have been on a walk. Anurati, without arguing, said yes, to what he asked. Ardhendu mentioned to her that he had a severe headache and he was unable to recall what he was thinking all the way from Dr. Saxena's clinic until he reached home. Anurati stopped for a second and asked why he went to Dr. Saxena's clinic when they had an appointment the coming week.

"No it was a casual visit and yes, do you want me to stay in this car forever or what?" Ardhendu pushed open his car door and stood outside. They then went inside the house. Ardhendu sat on the couch, as if relaxing after running a marathon. He closed his eyes and leaned his tired head against the couch, asking for a glass of chilled water. Anurati was already holding a glass of chilled water but was confused, whether to ask him or to let it go. She could not decide whether it was a panic attack, which was a symptom of his phobia or if it was just because of a sleepless night. "No I can't leave this matter like this," she spoke to herself, which was bit louder than usual.

"Did you say something?" Ardhendu asked.

"No I was… yes, I just…"

"Are you fine? What yes, no?" Ardhendu asked.

"I just wanted to know, is everything fine? You look very tired and worried."

"I am absolutely fine and yes, let us eat together," Ardhendu walked upstairs, signalling to Anurati that he would be working from home that day. Anurati was not as excited as she always was when her husband worked from home. She was tensed about Ardhendu's condition and state of his mind. She wondered if he was the same, sweet Ardhendu or was that he had started with his phobia again. The relapse of his Haphephobia would not be good. Anurati thought Ardhendu was a bright student, and that could have done something extraordinary for him. But he was content with what he did in life and what he earned for himself and his family. Anurati was an educated housewife. She dreamed of working and earning but destiny had never given her a chance to do so. After her BPT degree, i.e., the Bachelor's Degree in Physiotherapy, and knowing about Ardhendu's mental illness, she was busy taking care of her husband, his treatments and therapies as she believed Ardhendu's only cause of the phobia was because of her. She blamed herself for Ardhendu's fear and with time, Anurati decided to dedicate her entire life to him. Suddenly, the whistle of the pressure cooker filled the air.

"What's that?" The weight of the pressure cooker fell on the ground with a thud, bringing Anurati back from the old memories, right to her condominium's ultra-modular kitchen. Anurati was still tensed and unmindfully, she picked up the weight from the ground and put it back on the cooker. After a few hours Ardhendu seemed normal, with no sign or symptoms, so she came upstairs to check on him.

"Come on Aru, take some rest. You have been working for long. Sitting in front of your laptop and hitting the keyboard," Anurati teased Ardhendu by gently giving him a shoulder massage.

"Listen, I am not hitting my keyboard. I am working on an important project."

"Yes, I understand that. I don't work in the IT sector, but that doesn't mean I don't understand what you guys do! You simply press '*Enter*' and draw a handsome salary at the month end of each month!" she teased.

"Software engineers work on problems where there is a specific cost, a performance, and hardware, power and temperature and timing constraints. Issues such as user interface and considerations such as Google's Material Design are not the typical concerns of a software engineer. Is that clear, Anu?"

"That makes sense," Anurati closed her lips with a broad smile, nodding at what Ardhendu said.

"Anu, you know, software engineering isn't all about the code. It is all about how you go about getting the job done.

Of course, by pressing your so called '*Enter*' button," Ardhendu said and got up from his seat, hugged Anurati tight, locking his lips on hers. Anurati felt his hardness under her. This kiss from Ardhendu could not erase Anurati's worries. She thought of calling the doctor's clinic later, and asking what had frightened Ardhendu. She was sure that Ardhendu must have encountered something which had triggered his fear from deep within and that she would find out for sure.

The couple was normal by the evening but both of them were lost in thought. Ardhendu was tensed about telling her about Aniket's death and Anurati was tensed about the afternoon's incident. The love between them was so deep that none of them thought of hurting the other with sad news. Later that night, Ardhendu asked Anurati if she had received a call from anyone in India. Anurati said no, reminding Ardhendu about Aniket leaving for a seven-day vacation with his friend. No other relatives ever called her. Even Aniket had mentioned that he wouldn't be reachable, so he could talk only upon his return. "Status and photographs on Facebook will let us know where he is!" Anurati said, while both of them were sipping from their glasses. Earlier, it was coffee, but now it was skimmed milk for Anurati due to her pregnancy. Ardhendu didn't let her drink coffee.

"You remember Aru, we went to the same place for our honeymoon?" she kept talking, without letting Ardhendu speak. Ardhendu listened silently. Though he was physically present, his heart, mind and soul was far away, crying for what had happened to his brother-in-law. He was battling within and was still unsure as to how Anurati would react to the news of Aniket's death. With these thoughts, sweat rolled off his temple, which Anurati saw and wiped with her palm.

"Aru, are you feeling hot? Are you thinking of something?"

"No, no… I just sipped this very hot coffee and I burnt my tongue, see?" Ardhendu stuck his tongue out and showed it to Anurati as if to tease her.

"Show me, show me," said Anurati, and caught hold of his tongue with her fingers like a clamp holding an object.

"Yuck! Silly girl, holding my tongue with your dirty hands."

"Oh ho, Mishra *Ji*, is it? When you lick my tongue that is fine but if I am touching it is not?"

Anurati tried to keep the atmosphere cosy as she could guess that something serious had happened which was making Ardhendu behave differently. He was sweating even when he was sitting in the patio with the cool breeze blowing. Anurati was aware that his phobia could recur at any time if he had met those disturbing circumstances that disturbed the neural circuits in his brain, causing it to create bad images and pictures again, and making the patient fearful. Ardhendu was a haphephobic patient – fear of touch, quite rare amongst all phobias. *"For those who are affected, however, it can be devastating to both, their romantic and non-romantic lives. Most people who cannot trace their haphephobia to a specific event develop the fear early on in childhood, although it can manifest at any time."* This was what going on in Anurati's mind. But she had a very positive attitude towards life. She took everything well and decided that by hook or by crook, she would peep into his brain but wouldn't let him suffer the way he suffered few years ago. It was out of guilt that she had married Ardhendu, but deep down, in her heart, she was an "*Indian wife*". Now that she was his life partner, it was her duty to sail the boat to shore and not let it sink in between.

"I love you," said Anurati all of a sudden looking into Ardhendu's eyes. She knew that how much she meant by these three words now, more than ever before.

"I love you too, Sweetu. Do I need to say this to you?"

"Of course, you have to and you should. How else will I know that I am still in your heart?" Anurati winked at Ardhendu. They smiled at each other. They sat for another half-an-hour before drifting off to sleep.

CHAPTER FOUR

Trip to Jagatsinghpur, Odisha; May 1997

It was mid-May and the summer holidays had begun. As usual, Anurati and Aniket visited their grandparents at Sathalpur, a small village in Jagatsinghpur District, every year, during their vacations. This time, it was different. Ardhendu came with them. His father was busy with some official work and asked Anurati's father to take him along with his kids to his native if at all he was comfortable with that. With the news of *Bhaiya* accompanying them, Aniket was super excited. However, Anurati was not. She was scared of Ardhendu and of her feelings for him. She felt secure, friendly, and cool, whenever she was with Ardhendu, which made her explain every detail of how and what Rout Uncle had once done to her. She had hid it from her mother but she had very comfortably explained everything to Ardhendu. She felt that she was not able to resist herself from smiling, laughing and chatting with him for long hours whenever they were together and alone. She was too young to understand that destiny had a name for their friendship later in life.

Ardhendu accompanied them without any hesitation. He had clear feelings for Anurati. He saw her as a very special friend. He was always ready to do whatever she asked, and he listened to whatever she said. He even felt like family, with Aniket, but had absolutely no sibling-like feelings for Anurati. He didn't have any nasty thoughts for her, though, but was very caring and extra- protective towards her. The trip to their village, that too, with Aniket and Anurati, was the icing on the cake. He didn't have to spend his vacations all alone, with his gadgets back in Rourkela. It was a long trip, lasting nearly a month. He was desperately waiting for the day.

It was an overnight train journey from Rourkela to Cuttack and then a trip by car to Sathalpur, which was in the outskirts of Jagatsinghpur, about ten kilometres away. The greenery everywhere and the cool breeze from the taxi window was a heavenly feeling for Ardhendu. He was seeing a village for the first time. Cattles in the field; naked kids running along black tyres by hitting it with sticks in hand; young ladies, half-naked with their petticoats tied just above their chests, and bathing under water-taps outside their houses – it was a great sight. Ardhendu stared at everything with his eyes and mouth wide open. He saw Anurati's father waving at every person they passed by. Anurati's mother had wrapped the *pallu* of her sari over her head. This was her way of showing respect towards her in-laws. Or, she was forced to do so. This didn't matter to anyone inside the car. But, Anurati's father was very content with what his wife did. He felt as if his family was still grounded to traditions and culture, and that they respected his parents and his birthplace. He understood that they were born and brought up in an urban setting and things were different there.

Soon, they entered through a wooden gate and the taxi came to a halt. Anurati's father was the first to get out of the taxi. Every single member of the family stood outside to welcome them. This wasn't a usual phenomenon in cities. Bending half way and stretching his arm, he touched the feet of his parents and elders. Now it was Anurati's mother's turn. She was the daughter-in-law, so she kneeled down and touched her head at her father-in-law's feet and gradually sought blessings in descending order of age, from the other members. For a few minutes, it went on like this. The elders blessed her, and the younger ones sought her blessings. Ardhendu was not part of these customs. He stood near the taxi door, holding it open and was busy watching everyone. Everyone seemed excited. Ardhendu had never seen such a big family with so many members. Ardhendu heard Anurati's father explain to his father, "Yes, of course! A Brahmin boy! Or else, I would never had asked him to accompany us to this place."

"Okay, then let him come in," somebody in the crowd said. Anurati protested against what she heard. "Tell me, grandfather, what if he wasn't of caste?"

"Just shut up Anu," whispered Anurati's mother from behind.

"But mamma..." her father didn't let her complete the sentence and made a loud noise, accusing his elder brother, wondering if he would let them get inside the house or they would be there forever. Everybody laughed at what he said and they entered. There were servants to pick their luggage, sweets and snack boxes and fruit baskets which were stuffed inside the boot space of the taxi. Anurati was embarrassed and came to Ardhendu, and tried consoling him. "I am sorry, Ardhendu. Don't mind what these people think and say. We are here to have fun!" She apologized on behalf of her parents, who didn't protest against this behaviour.

"Hey, Anu I understand completely. Don't worry about me. And, yes nobody did anything wrong, so no need of any sorry!"

Aniket pulled Ardhendu forcefully by his hand, taking him inside the house. It was very different in structure when compared to houses in cities. There was an open space in the centre, called the '*Aangan.*' There were rooms all around it. "Come on Aru bhaiya, this is our room! We shall share the room for twenty days. Let me make one thing clear, no one is ever going to say you anything. Always remember, when I am here, no fear!" All three of them laughed aloud. Aniket hit his fists on his not-so-broad chest like a gorilla. After some time, Anurati went to Aniket and asked about her elder cousin, Geetu, whom she could not find anywhere. Aniket was busy playing marbles with his friends and said he had not seen her anywhere, either. Ardhendu heard the name for the first time and didn't bother to respond to what both brother and sister spoke about. Anurati moved from one room to another to find her, as she thought she must be playing a prank on her. They were good friends and shared almost everything. Once each year, they met in the summer holidays and chatted a lot on every topic they felt like: happenings, village affairs, boys and lots more. Anurati was eager to meet her when she heard one of her aunties speak to her mother, saying that Geetu was in the dark room, next to the cattle shed, for two days. She heard her mother say that today was the last day for her to remain there, secluded from everyone else. Anurati understood what it meant, so she went away to her room that she and Geetu used to share every year.

"Dark room? During menses? Why? I was not treated like this when I had my periods!" Anurati was disturbed with what she heard but didn't dare ask anyone. This was embarrassing and disgusting for her to discuss. She was happy that Geetu would be back the next day.

Now, it was time for lunch. Back in Rourkela, everyone sat together for lunch, and the whole family would sit together on weekends. It was called the Sunday Lunch, and special dishes were cooked by her mother. But here, the concept was different. Male members, both young and old, were served first. They would eat, chatting, laughing and munching for an hour or so. All the best portions of the food along with fresh ripe fruits were served. They were supposed to eat to their hearts content. Everyone seemed to be enjoying the food, but from a corner, Anurati saw her father making signalling to her mother that he had left some good pieces of mutton for her, and two very sweet slices of mango. Anurati was delighted to see this and was very happy that her father was so loving and caring for her mother. Usually, in some families, daughters-in-law are neglected this way. No one is bothered to see whether the lady who was serving the food has her share of food or not.

"Why don't you finish your food? You seemed to have changed a lot after staying in the city! You don't seem to be eating properly," shouted Anurati's grandmother.

"My stomach had shrunk, *Bou!* If I take another bite from this, I will burst. I know you won't like that." Anurati's father laughed out loud. He got up to wash his hands, following his father. After that, everyone started getting up in turns, and went to where the maid was pouring water from a *lota*, a small spherical water vessel usually made up of brass, to wash their hands. It looked like a custom and tradition to Ardhendu. But Aniket and Anurati were used to this but they don't like this. They were nurtured, with a belief that both men and women were the same and deserved an equal position in society and should be treated equally. Both mother and father, are the same in every respect. The sound of a hungry stomach is the same for both bodies. So why should a husband eat first and a wife be forced to eat in the same plate, after? She kept asking her mother this. Her mother explained that it was out of love and respect for her husband and Anurati wouldn't understand this now.

"Whose plate are you going to use, Anu?"

"Shut up!" Anurati was hungry and the smell of the cooked food made it worse. She pulled her mother who was busy wiping Aniket's hand with a *Gamucha*, a coarse, traditional cotton towel found in India and Bangladesh used to dry one's body. It was half past two now. Both Aniket and Ardhendu went for an afternoon nap. Anurati, while crossing them, holding her mother's hand on her left, signalled to Ardhendu with her right hand from her mouth to her stomach as if asking whether he had his food. She even rubbed her belly as if asking whether it is full or not. Aniket saw this and thought she was asking him.

"You saw both of us eating and again you are asking whether we had our food or not?" Aniket shouted at Anurati.

Ardhendu blinked and smiled at what just happened and winked at her. He was happy that Anurati was so caring. He was sure that she must have understood that he answered her question by blinking his eyes.

Now that all the male members were gone, Anurati's aunt took out a rusty aluminium saucer with cooked food in it and started walking towards the dark room. All the ladies were whispering and Anurati, who sat very close, could not hear what they were talking about. But she didn't dare to ask anyone. She knew they all were talking about those dirty days. She saw her aunt come back in no time.

"Did you tell your daughter to finish her food and wash the plate?" asked Anurati's grandmother.

"Yes, *Bou* and I also told her to get up early tomorrow before sunrise and bathe with turmeric water."

"Oh, yes! Three days are over. Good that you reminded me."

All of a sudden, grandmother asked Anurati's mother about her menarche. But to her surprise, her mother very politely lied that she had not yet started with her periods. She was surprised to what her mother replied but didn't interrupt as she used to do on every other issue. After eating, she washed her hands by pouring water from the *lota* as everyone else did and she went straight to her mother and wiped her wet hands in her *pallu.* There wasn't a pipeline or taps anywhere. There was a tube-well and a well with a pulley to take out water and use. It was a sunny day and after a very heavy meal Anurati waved goodbye to her mother and went straight to nap. She was all alone and was missing Geetu. She kept thinking why Geetu was placed there in a dark room like a prisoner. If she had her periods, it wasn't her fault! It was a biological clock that struck and she had stepped over from childhood to adulthood, that was it! What's the big deal in that? All these thoughts knocked about in her head but she could not ask anyone. She could not argue about it either. Her mother already lied that she hadn't had hers. Why did her mother lie? With these controversies in her mind she fell asleep.

"Anu, Anu… get up you lazy girl!" Aniket pulled Anurati by her arms. She was fast asleep. Aniket started tickling her and made wake up. Anurati rubbed her eyes and saw Aniket and Ardhendu in front of her.

"Get up Anu. Let's go to the playground. We shall climb trees and pluck some mangoes." Last year, she had a lot of fun together. She played marbles, *guchu-dandu*, rolled thin black tyres running from one place to another, learning swimming in pond water, diving from a high level straight into the middle of the water, caught fishes and lots more.

"No Aniket. You both carry on," sleepy Anurati replied.

"Come on, please. Be sporty. We shall have fun together," pleaded Aniket and again tried pulling Anurati by her hand and this time it was hard in order to make her stand.

"Oh, leave me alone. You are hurting me Aniket."

Seeing this, Ardhendu tried handling the situation. "Hey Aniket, come let's go and ride that big *Atlas bicycle*. I will teach you to ride it from under the railings. It is called half-riding."

"Half-riding, what is that Bhaiya?"

"Come with me first, I will show you."

Both the boys left the room and Anurati lay flat on her bed with a thin sheet over herself. She stared at the ceiling fan which was spinning at high speed but was so slow that she could easily see and count the number of blades due to very low voltage. She thought about her conversation with Aniket. "Why did I shout at Aniket? He only asked me to join him and play. I should not have done this!"

She got up immediately, tied her hair into a pony tail with the rubber band on the dressing table, as dowry brought by her mother at the time of her wedding. She knew that her mother was very proud of the teakwood dressing table and always taunted her father about the expensive things she had brought along with her at the time of her wedding. Anurati checked herself in the mirror and rushed out of the room, and out of the main door. She could see Aniket and Ardhendu riding big bicycles by putting the legs from under the front rod and holding the handle with one hand and the other hand was on the rod, as they were pedalling fast. Unknowingly, she stared at Ardhendu and was admiring him, wondering how cool he was. He managed Aniket well. She waved at the boys, smiled to herself and went back to her room. Anurati was spending time all alone, so time seemed to be moving slowly. Now that it was dusk, the ladies made tea while chatting with each other and her grandma did the evening *Poojan* by putting cotton wick to fire at the *Tulsi* plant in front of the house. She even banged the *Ghanta*. Everyone gathered for tea. The ladies were fully dedicated to the household chores including making dinner, which they had very early. Anurati was no longer interested in listening to whispers anymore. She finished her food and ran to Aniket to talk to him.

"Hey, Aniket! Did you learn how to half-ride?"

"Yes, I did. It is so exciting. I will teach you tomorrow, don't worry!"

"You had your dinner? Did you find Geetu?" Ardhendu asked Anurati.

"Yes, I had my dinner…okay, goodnight," Anurati hurriedly answered and ran out of the room. She didn't want to lie to Ardhendu about Geetu. She could not explain where and how she was. If at all she explained it to Ardhendu, she wouldn't be able to handle Aniket and his mysterious questions.

"See, what happened to her manners and etiquette. She ran away without even answering to what you have asked."

"It's okay, Aniket! She must be tired. Let's sleep, we have to get up early to watch the sunrise at the bank of the river," said Ardhendu, in an authoritarian voice.

"That will be exciting, Bhaiya, goodnight." Gradually they fell asleep.

Anurati was moving from one room to other, chatting with her aunties and mother. She heard her father calling her. He wanted to introduce Anurati to his math teacher, an old man in his mid-fifties. Her father said rather proudly, "Meet Shiva Prasad Sir, our Mohanty Sir, as we call him." He asked Anurati to touch his feet and seek his blessings. Anurati did exactly as her father said and sat beside her *grandfather*. Mohanty Sir was also her grandpa's friend. After a few minutes of chatting, Anurati's father had to leave as his friends had come to talk with him. All of a sudden, Anurati's grandpa had a coughing fit and he walked out fast to spit out the sputum and clear his throat. Now that Anurati was alone with Mohanty Sir in a dimly lit room, Mohanty Sir took a few steps towards her and sat beside her, almost touching his thighs against hers. Anurati instantly reacted to what he did and folded her legs, one over the other. However, the man caught hold of her thighs and started rubbing and pressing them hard. His touch made her very uncomfortable. She wanted to run away from him, but flashes of the past, what Rout Uncle had done once, kept creeping up in her mind and she was left sitting there, unmindful and scared.

"So? You cute little girl, you are in Standard IX?" asked Mohanty Sir, with his hands on her thighs.

"No, Standard VII. Classes will start after vacations," Anurati answered with arrogance, and as rudely as she could.

"Okay, so you are in Class VII but you look as if…" Mohanty Sir observed her very closely. "How was your mathematics paper? How much did you score this time?" now that he was busy asking questions, he moved his hands closer to Anurati's trouser pockets as if doing unintentionally.

"I scored ninety-three out of hundred. I am sleepy," Anurati tried getting up. But to her surprise Mohanty Sir dug his right hand inside her trouser pocket and tried pulling out a key-chain. "Enough!" said Anurati, loud and clear. She snatched her Vicks inhaler key-chain back from him, stood up and headed straight out of the room and collided with her grandpa.

"I am sorry, grandpa! Please excuse me. Goodnight," she said and ran out of the room.

"Hey! How is your cough? We have grown old now!" said Mohanty Sir as if everything was normal and that he was concerned for his friend. Grandpa tried asking why Anurati had run away and he said that he heard her say something. He explained that Anurati was happy that she scored good marks and he told his friend that he would teach Anurati some complex formulae to help her in higher classes and laughed out loud.

"Of course, you should teach these kids. If you agree, I shall arrange for you to take classes in a day or two!" Anurati's grandpa was unaware of what his sick friend was trying to do to her.

Anurati was disturbed by what had just happened. This was the second time that somebody tried taking advantage of her and had touched her without her consent. It made her feel uncomfortable. She could hardly sleep and kept turning and twisting in bed. She could not imagine why these elders were doing such bad things. What was so tempting in her that they were forgetting the relationships they shared with her, and more importantly, the age gap? Every time she closed her eyes, she could feel his touch and it made her feel weak. She covered herself with a sheet from head to toe, despite the hot weather and tried chanting the *Hanuman Chalisa* to get some strength and some sleep. She slept, but was awakened by a cold touch at her feet. She was terrified to feel someone very close to her back and hands over her waist inside her sheet. Out of fear, she could not shout. She didn't dare to move her legs and arms. She was as stiff as a dead person. She wondered what would happen if this hand started brushing her breasts. What if this hand started moving under her pants? She started sweating and panting. Her heartbeat was audible in her ears.

"Hey, Rati, you got up so early! Turn to me," Geetu was excited to see Anurati awake.

"Huh! It's you. Thank god."

"Why are you so scared? You are safe and secure here. Who else shall come under your sheet? You seem to have become naughty in a year." Anurati didn't answer, but turned towards Geetu and hugged her tight, as if she was a child clinging to her mother.

"I missed you so much. Why you were in that isolated room? I heard you had your first..." Anurati stopped short, putting her tongue in between her teeth.

"I had what? It seems you had yours, if I am not wrong, Rati? You can always share with me!"

"I am scared to tell you as my mother lied to grandma that I didn't have mine yet."

"Shut up! You hid it from me too!" Geetu tried explaining how a girl is treated when she gets her first menses. She said it was humiliating. She explained that people threw big receptions, inviting friends and relatives in order to announce that their girl had grown up and that she was no longer a baby to play with dolls, and announce that she can deliver babies.

"So you knew about this earlier?"

"I attended two or three reception parties two weeks ago. So I was aware of what they were up to. You know, sometimes I feel jealous of you. You are so lucky to stay away from such traditions and customs..."

Anurati was not listening to what Geetu was saying. She remembered her mother saying that she should stay away from boys mostly because she had her periods. But she didn't know what that meant. So by listening to Geetu's explanation she was scared of her last two touches where both of them tried touching her at wrong places. "Let me know one thing, if I touch someone with my hand then will I get pregnant?"

"*Nah re*, Silly! It should be a proper touch. Front to front." Geetu pulled Anurati and hugged her giving a demo for what she called a *proper touch*.

"Okay, now I can relax."

"Wait a second, why are you so tensed about touch and all… has something happened?" Anurati tried explaining that she was educating herself and that there was nothing much to tell her. "Listen, Rati, you know your name can attract *Kamdeva*, the Hindu god of human love or desire? So beware!"

Both of them giggled, teased and tickled each other but Anurati was really tensed about what Geetu had just said. Half her name was after *Kamdeva's* wife's name, was it the reason why she was encountering such sick people? Unaware and uneducated about touch and hugging, Anurati tried to stay brave and vehemently refused her grandpa when he proposed that she take tuitions from Mohanty Sir. Luckily, her parents listened to what she said and thought it would be wise to let the kids enjoy their vacations. All four kids once went to a mango orchard where Aniket and Geetu climbed the tree. Ardhendu and Anurati were standing below to collect the fruits. Anurati was actually looking for a chance to talk to Ardhendu, which she didn't get when at home. "You know, last night, that *idiot* misbehaved with me. He pressed my thigh and would have gotten up to some mischief, but I ran away."

"Who was that? What are you talking about?" Ardhendu was worried about what he had heard. He looked high up, but could not find Aniket and Geetu because of the dense branches. He was sure that they were somewhere far to hear the conversation.

"Mohanty *budha*."

Ardhendu was tensed and started pacing up and down. He could not speak. He wanted to kill someone. He started sweating and closed both his fist as if he was ready to punch something. His face turned red. "I shall chop off his hands"

Anurati got scared of such a vision and caught hold of his right fist. "Cool down. What is the matter? Are you alright? I am fine…I told you that I ran away!"

Within a few minutes, Ardhendu seemed to be back to normal to Anurati. Both the other kids had gotten down from the trees. As usual, Aniket started dividing the fruits amongst them. Earlier, it was three equal portions, but this time it was amongst four. They all seemed busy with the ripe mangoes but Anurati was disturbed at how Ardhendu had behaved some few minutes ago. But she didn't dare to ask Ardhendu. She tried taking extra care from then onwards whenever she got a chance. Days passed and it was soon the last night that both Geetu and Anurati were together, they decided to talk all night instead of wasting time sleeping.

"Rati, tell me, what is it that you like in Ardhendu?"

"What is there to like or dislike? He is just a good friend, simple."

"But I smell something fishy in your friendship. You care for him and behave so differently when you are with him. I even saw your eyes dancing with happiness when you stood near him. Tell me, I will keep it as a secret. Mother promise!" Geetu pinched her throat to enforce her point.

"*Nah re*, nothing special. But I can say he is a nice boy. You already know about his family. So I feel sad for him."

"But you can try your luck for love. He is so good looking and rich. Rati, I am saying that you are missing a lovely chance by not choosing him as a boyfriend, but if you tell me, I can try him as…" before Geetu could complete her sentence Anurati cut in her words without letting her speak much.

"*Huh,* Shut up!" This time Anurati was loud and clear. Both the girls chatted till they drifted off to sleep. Anurati did not love Ardhendu. She was too young to understand her feelings for him. But there was no doubt that she shared a very special bond with him that made her comfortable whenever she was around him. Ardhendu, on the other hand, was quite clear about his feelings. He cared for Anurati whenever he had a chance. He helped Anurati whenever he could. Now that she was sharing secrets with him he thought he had booked a special place for himself in her heart. They had no idea of the game that destiny was playing with them, as it was still unknown that they were future soul-mates.

CHAPTER FIVE

Edison, New Jersey; September 2014

Anurati later called her doctor's clinic and knew that Ardhendu had met his psychiatrist. It made him think of his past and what he had suffered. She took it casually and relaxed. The day arrived for the scheduled appointment at the doctor's clinic. She tried convincing Ardhendu that she would manage alone and that he need not come along but she failed. They got ready to visit the doctor. Neither Anurati nor Ardhendu spoke about the phone call or the visit to doctor's clinic, respectively. Anurati was scared that he might meet his psychiatrist again and that he would be in trouble. But as she had not told him about the phone call, she could not refuse Ardhendu's offer to join her at the hospital. She was scared of hurting him, albeit unintentionally. She was spying on him and had tried finding out his whereabouts. Sometimes, silence is the best option for certain issues. She tried staying calm and quiet. Ardhendu was not aware of Anurati's thoughts. He was determined to let his wife know about Aniket's accident. He thought everybody would be there at the clinic to look after his wife and his unborn child. Anurati would also understand why he didn't let her know about the accident earlier. They were both busy with their thoughts and kept things a secret from each other, purely out of their love for each other. There were no other ulterior motives.

At the clinic, the caregiver lubricated the Foetal Doppler with the ultrasound gel and started rubbing it around Anurati's belly. As it was early on in the pregnancy, the caregiver moved the transducer on the midline of her abdomen, above the pubic line, aiming downward behind the pubic bone and then searched for the foetal heartbeat. Since the foetal heart tends to be small at this stage of pregnancy, they could only hear a very faint heartbeat. Both, Ardhendu and Anurati were happy to listen to their baby's heartbeat. For a moment, they were lost and everything around them seemed ecstatic. Anurati was still lying on the side bed when Ardhendu went to her and said, "You know Anu, how much I love you? You know..."

"Yes darling, what is the matter? You need not have to explain your love to me. It is already within me and I am feeling it," she caught hold of his palm and rubbed it along her bare abdomen.

"Just listen and please don't take me otherwise. You just think that what all I did was because I love you and I care for you and our baby. I cannot live without you, or say if anything happens to you!"

"Aru, please let me know what the matter is? What is wrong with you? I said I can feel your love deep in my heart." Now that Ardhendu was in tears, Anurati, with the help of a nurse, got off the bed and was about to get down when Ardhendu went straight to her and caught hold of her. "Listen, you have to be bold enough to listen to what I am going to disclose," he was loud and clear, almost yelling.

"Are you alright?"

"Yes, I am fine but somebody else is not."

"Is our baby alright? Are there any complications with my pregnancy?"

"God, damn it! Will you just shut up, Anu? There is something else in this world, beyond me, beyond our baby. Do you know Aniket is no more? He had an accident on his way to..."

"What? No more... accident... Aniket..." Anurati could hardly say these words and fainted back from where she was sitting.

"Anu, Anu..." Ardhendu kept shaking and shouted, "Doctor, doctor..." Soon, nurses and the doctor took over. They asked Ardhendu to step outside, and to calm down and not worry. Anurati's pounding chest suggested that she was alive. She was in shock but was not dead. Ardhendu seemed relaxed that everything was taken care of. Now that he had disclosed the news about Aniket's passing, he was relaxed and no longer guilty.

"She just fainted out of shock," said the doctor. Again the Doppler was used and with the baby's heartbeat, quite clear this time, everything seemed normal. The sound of the heartbeat made Anurati speak out. "My baby, my baby!" she brushed her palm over her belly. Tears rolled down her cheeks. She was uncontrollable. Anurati was struck dumb.

"Anurati, I must say you are a brave soul and a lucky one with a husband who is always with you!" Anurati looked at Ardhendu, who was beside her, smiling. "I must remind you, Anurati. Your husband cared for you and your baby so much that he met me last week and we discussed this on the phone."

"Yes doctor," Anurati said and looked blankly at her husband.

"So Anurati knew that he came to the clinic but didn't enquire about this. What made her do so?' Ardhendu thought. Now that doctor disclosed the phone call, Anurati wondered why the doctor had said anything. Both remained silent with their thoughts.

"Eat healthy, stay healthy. And yes, Anurati, I am sorry again about your brother but it is destiny. So try relaxing and don't stress yourself." The doctor said, scribbling some medicine names in the prescription for Anurati and prepared herself to see the next patient. On their way home, they didn't utter a single word. Both thought themselves guilty in their own ways. But no one was guilty. Out of love, out of fear of losing the other, they kept things to themselves. Now that everything was out in the open, no one was able to muster enough courage to shatter the stillness between them. For the first time after so many years there was a long pause between the two. It was a smooth ride from hospital to home. Ardhendu had already worked for the day and the other half he was on leave. It was Ardhendu who broke the silence and was the first to speak.

"Anu, I am sorry. I know..."

"No, Aru. I am really sorry. I should have asked you why you came to the clinic and what was the matter that kept you so tensed and worried for so many days. I should have read your heart. You always loved me more than I loved you," she kept saying and sobbing. Ardhendu could hardly complete his sentence.

"Come on, Anu! That's fine. Don't cry. Don't. Please. You know I can't see your tears. They break my heart and see, my hands..." Ardhendu showed his trembling hands to her which were clammy.

"See, I stopped crying. You don't worry. I am fine. I am absolutely fine, dear." Anurati instantly wiped her tears and smiled at Ardhendu. Deep in her heart she could feel the pain of losing her only brother. She could feel the pain that Ardhendu had, for having hidden the truth from her since so many days. She thought she was brave. "Aru, out of love you didn't say anything. I understand. And I did not enquire with you as I was scared of asking you. I thought you might feel that I was spying on you and not trusting you. So I thought of waiting till you spoke up. You even met your psychiatrist and..."

"Oh, yes, I met with him and you know..." Ardhendu was interrupted with his wife's lips. Anurati kissed him hard and strong, with her heart, body, mind and soul. It was a long one, as if saying, "Oh, darling – you love me. You love me so much. But my love for you – oh, my god. How can I ever forgive myself for not loving you so dearly and selflessly? It was out of guilt that I married you but it was only love for which you married me." As if listening to her heart Ardhendu pulled himself from her lock. He hugged her tight, but with extra care, and said, "Anu, you know, I am grateful that you are my wife. I have loved you since our school days. I can't even imagine myself with any other girl. I was even struggling with serious phase of haphephobia but it was you who supported me and brought me out of that fear." Ardhendu kept blabbering when Anurati again lost in her thoughts. She thought how the incidents of her life and her childhood troubles made him feel forlorn and helpless that he developed his fear of touch. After going through so much in life he was still grateful for marrying her. She felt lucky for having gotten a caring and loving husband like Ardhendu who was madly in love with her and always loved her more than she did.

"Anu, Anu... have you slept?" shaking her from her thoughts Ardhendu asked.

"No, No, I was listening to you." Anurati was speechless with what was going on all around her. Now that she was with Ardhendu and was bearing his child, she felt she was on cloud nine and the luckiest women on earth. They chatted for long about Aniket. Anurati tried being cheerful for the sake of her baby and husband. The thought of Aniket made her weak but she did not have the choice of shedding tears. She was scared that it might hurt her baby and tried distracting herself from that thought. A few days had passed. As per Hindu cremation rituals, her uncle and cousins took charge after being informed by Ardhendu. She came to know that there was nothing much to do with Aniket's last rites as the intensity of accident had charred the body, completely leaving nothing except black ashes. But cremation was a formality and it was done back at her grandparents' place. She was still and was only blankly listening to what Ardhendu told her. Aniket's death left a big void in her heart. Her world was now Ardhendu and her unborn baby and she had to take extra care for these two lives. Now, she realized how much she loved him. She thought she would never let him suffer any more. She would love him more than he loved. What if days have passed, yet there are many more years ahead. She promised herself that she would fill Ardhendu's life with surprises and make him feel special someday, and then one day, she could proudly say, "*I hold my breath for you* and can even die for you, my love."

The weather was cool. There were no more secrets to be unfolded. There was no more guilt. Destiny has its own way of unfolding. The only thing that mattered now was the baby: six more months for the baby to come to this world. "See?" Ardhendu asked Anurati, gesturing to her to look at the kitchen cabinets, the walls and doors where he had pasted cute baby printouts with one-liners like "Eat healthy and stay healthy." This brought a smile in Anurati's face after a long time. Moving along with Ardhendu and looking at cute baby pictures and discussing the looks of the baby, she saw her phone ring. She asked him to bring her the phone before the call was disconnected.

"What? I don't understand what you are pointing at?" Ardhendu shouted at Anurati, who was sipping from her sipper. With a big gulp, she said, "My phone! It's on silent mode, I guess! Please get it fast!" Before Ardhendu could reach to the mobile the call was missed. "Who's that?" she was impatient to know who the caller was.

"It's Lisa," Ardhendu gave the mobile to her and went upstairs.

"I am making a call, you..." Before Anurati could complete her sentence, Ardhendu asked her to take her time and that he would look into his office work for a while. Anurati called India. Lisa was on vacation to Rourkela and was to be back to her job in NJ, within a month. She was the one who had given the news to Ardhendu that night about the accident and Aniket. But Ardhendu and she made a plan together, to not tell Anurati this at that time. They decided to look for the proper time and place to do it. She stopped calling Anurati from that day onwards, till she received the message from Ardhendu that Anurati was aware of her brother's death and she made the call today. "I don't want to talk to you," was the first thing Anurati said and remained silent on the phone.

"Is it? Sorry, I was..." before Lisa could say anything, Anurati told her about Aniket and finally broke down. Soon, she consoled herself, looking at the pictures around her that Ardhendu had pasted to help her remain cheerful and stress free. Anurati smiled at herself and they had a long chat almost for an hour before she hung up. With the end of the call, Ardhendu thanked Lisa from the bottom of his heart and cherished the friendship. Friends are real treasures and should be preserved! Anurati sat on her sofa, recollecting Lisa's words, 'All you have in this world is Ardhendu and your baby.' Lisa was right!

Slowly, she got off her seat and walked to her bedroom. Climbing a few steps, she recalled the other thing that Lisa said. Her head started reeling, as if everything around her had begun rotating. Lisa said something about '*MG*'! He was in NJ for about six months for some research! Anurati thought, 'Why on earth is he here? Why not some other state or some other planet? What next?' Anurati caught hold of her head with both hands and gradually started moving down the stairs before she fell and met with an accident. She went back and leaned her head back on the couch. She was restless. It was something big this time. How can she explain to Ardhendu, if by any chance they both meet with each other? She thought of lots of things. She thought she won't let Ardhendu go out for six months' but how was that possible?

"No, not this..." Anurati spoke out loudly. She thought of calling Lisa... "No, not now. Let her comeback to NJ. If I say something now this will only complicate things." She again spoke to herself loudly. She thought of contacting *MG* and letting him know that she and Ardhendu were in NJ and asking him to stay away from her life and carry on his research somewhere else. "How is that feasible? Who am I to tell him this? Why will he listen to me?"

"Yes, darling, I am at your service. I will listen to whatever you say," Ardhendu said so with a broad grin in his face.

"You are downstairs? What are you doing here?"

"What is the matter? Why are you so serious?"

Anurati cleverly smiled at him and narrated how she felt like she was fainting, while climbing the stairs. She explained how everything seemed to spin. Instead of moving up, she felt it would be better to walk down and rest. "And you thought you won't let me know this?" Ardhendu cut short her words and went straight to kitchen and grabbed a big glass of juice for her. "You are supposed to keep yourself hydrated! Every few hours, try drinking something. Keep doing this. Don't neglect your health!" said Ardhendu, in an authoritarian tone.

"Yes, my lord," Anurati smiled at him sipping the juice. In her mind, she thanked god some thousand times. She was happy that Ardhendu was still not aware of MG. But she did have to deal with this. The sooner she had to disclose it, the better it was. But now, they were tired and needed sleep.

CHAPTER SIX

Rourkela, Odisha; November 1997 – April 1999

Ardhendu collected the prints of the photographs he had taken during his summer trip, from the studio. On the way, he met Aniket. He waved at him and said he would meet him at the playground and rode as fast as he could, towards his house. There was a lot of excitement to see the photos. When he got them home, Ardhendu threw his shoes away and went straight to his room and locked it from inside. He wanted complete privacy. Slowly, he opened the envelope and found a handful of photos, all colourful and shiny. Two empty albums were also enclosed. He threw the albums to a side and lay down on his belly, spreading the photographs all over the bed. He kept himself busy for a few hours, just looking at the pictures. He searched for Anurati's picture and stared at it for a few minutes, which he couldn't do in reality. How could he stare at Anurati for so long? With her photo, though, he could easily do it! Holding one photo in his hand, he said, "Look Anu, I love you. I am madly in love with you. Look at me!" It was a picture he had taken when Anurati was telling him about Rout Uncle's act. A drizzle of sweat was also seen in the photograph, with her fearful big eyes. 'How scared she was, even while narrating the incident to me!' he thought. Ardhendu closed his fist hard and was filled with rage. He kissed those eyes in the photo. "Don't worry Anu, I am always with you and I will protect you all my life," he spoke loudly. He took another single photograph of Anurati. This photograph was taken when she was telling him about Mohanty Sir's actions. He could see the same fear in her eyes. He kissed the photograph on her lips. "You are so pretty! Nothing can touch you, that will harm you," He closed his fist and behaved as if he wants to kill someone. He hit his fist very hard to the wall, feeling hopeless and helpless in saving the love of his life.

Luckily, he was disturbed with a knock at his door. "Aru, Aru…are you sleeping? It's me!"

"Anu," Ardhendu shouted from inside. "One moment please!" He immediately put those two photographs under his mattress and then opened the door.

"What a pleasant surprise…" said Aru, and peeped behind her shoulders.

"Whom are your eyes searching for?"

"Aniket? He is not around. How come you are alone? That is unusual!"

"No, actually my mother had sent *laddus* for you. I could not find uncle and your maid said you were inside. So…"

"Oh, is it? Thank you, Aunty!" said Ardhendu delightfully and snatched the box from her hand.

"Did I disturb you?" Anurati behaved formally, although she didn't mean to be that formal.

"Come inside, I have a surprise for you."

"Wow, so many photographs. When did you get those rolls developed?"

"Now only I collected the printouts from the studio."

"How are the pictures?"

"You are beautiful. I mean they are beautiful," Ardhendu corrected himself.

"What? You saw them?"

"Yeah, just roughly," Ardhendu didn't mean to lie to her, but simply answered for the sake of making conversation.

"Please, can I take them? I will see them and return them to you."

"Hey, I got one set developed for you. I mean for Aniket. Take this whole packet."

"So sweet of you, thank you! The entire roll came up nicely! There are forty photographs, right?"

"No, I think thirty-eight out of forty. Two pictures are blacked out."

"Which one Aru?" Anurati asked, curious and worried about losing her favourite ones.

"Silly, Anu, how can I say which ones they were? They're blacked out right? So no image!"

"Okay, thank you. I must leave now."

"Why you are in a hurry? You can see the pictures here too. I mean, we can see them together."

Anurati denied staying there, and thanked him again for the extra copies that he had developed for Aniket and went out. Ardhendu kept staring at her, and was happy that she was so innocent and pure. He came back and took the two snaps from under his pillow and apologized that he had lied to her, but he couldn't even disclose his feelings to her. It would be too early to do that. He was a high school student and Anurati was a middle-school student.

"Knock! Knock!" said a voice from outside his room. He instantly pushed those two snaps under his pillow.

"Anu, you are here again?"

"Why? I can't be here?" said Anurati with a childish look and mischievous tone.

"You are always welcome. But let me warn you, knock before you enter and yes, I must also thank you that you did that."

"Oh, really, are you hiding something?" She asked as if she knew what he was doing before she entered the room.

"Yes… No… Actually…"

"Listen, I was just joking, but yes, I came to let you know that we will be out of station for my cousin's *thread ceremony*. We shall be back by Monday, and if not, by Tuesday for sure!" Without giving Ardhendu a chance, she said whatever she felt."Anyway, Aniket would have told me about this. He will be here in minutes!"

"Oh, is it? Then I must not have come back to let you know."

"Come on, Anu. It's not that…"

"It's okay. Just kidding!" Anurati winked at him and waved her hand and went away. The atmosphere was cool and cosy. Everything seemed to be nice to Ardhendu. The rest of his evening passed by very quickly. Even the days passed by very quickly, with only her thoughts. Even with Aniket, he felt very comfortable and cheerful, like he was family. But now, he missed Anurati, and *terribly*, at that.

"No Aru, don't touch me," said Anurati, screaming at top of her voice. She then pushed him back. "No, stop Aru! Please. You can't do this to me. You shouldn't!"

"But why?" asked Ardhendu, roaring at her. "But why can't I do this to you? Whoever feels like is touching you, rubbing your thighs, pressing your *breast*, then why shouldn't I?"

"What do you mean by why? I am telling you to stop coming on to me!" Anurati pleaded with folding hands, and tears were rolling down her chubby cheeks. Ardhendu kept pouncing on her until she finally hit her back against the wall in the room. Now that he knew she couldn't move an inch, he put his palm, cupping her breast as Rout Uncle did, that ominous night, and started pressing it. Before she could shout, he locked his lips hard against her with his erect instrument touching the space between her legs precisely, and she clung more onto the wall with his force.

Thud!

"Oh, it's so cold!" said Ardhendu, lying on the ground with only his T-shirt and his naked butt kissing the icy cold floor. He was surprised to see himself in this condition. He was half-naked, in the middle of the night. He quickly got up from the floor and hurriedly locked his door. He wrapped himself with his blanket and thought of the weirdest dream that he had just woken up from. He tried consoling himself that it was just a dream, but it was very difficult for him to relax, as he kept thinking. "Why on earth did I dream of molesting Anu?" He was disturbed, and kept thinking that it was lust. He didn't mean to hurt Anu in any way. He loved her. But with these bad images in his mind. He decided not to touch her. It might scare her, hurt her and she might not like this type of touch. He kept saying all these things, and pulled out the photographs and rubbed his finger above it. "I love you the way you are. I love the way you smile. I love the way you talk and *I hold my breaths for you.*"

Days passed. Seasons changed. Kids grew taller and the adults grew older. Everyone was in high school now. The heavy syllabus in CBSE schools, lesser in comparison with the ICSE ones, was a bit of a burden. There was hardly any time to play outside. Kids started leading monotonous lives. There were classes in the morning, followed by school, and then separate coaching classes for entrance examinations. Late at night, the students would go through the lessons they learned in class and then complete all their homework, do their practicals, and last but not the least, a huge amount of project work in almost every subject. If you want to be a good student, you have to work hard. The first duty of a student was to take tuitions from their school teacher. If they did not, there was a strict rule followed by a few teachers, not all, that the student was ignored completely inside the classroom. Anurati was aware of this and took tuitions from the hypocrites, not for the sake of knowledge, but for the sake of not being humiliated inside the classroom. Ardhendu guided her in every way he could, as though he was a mentor. Everyone in the colony liked Ardhendu more, when he succeeded with very good scores in the tenth standard board exams and then in the twelfth standard board exams, in the science stream, and finally cracked a seat in the Computer Science branch of the Rourkela Engineering College, now known as NIT, Rourkela, all in one shot. People respect education and getting admission in a reputed college was a different story altogether. Everybody praised the Mishra boy. They calculated the salary he would draw once he got into an MNC through his campus selections.

Ardhendu was a hero amongst the kids. Parents started making him an example. Anurati's parents were no different. She was made to follow his footsteps rather than fulfilling her wishes. Lisa and Anurati went to their coaching classes and tuitions and tried doing project work together. Aniket and Gourav were still young, but they concentrated on their studies more than wasting time in playing outside all the time. Parents seemed happy that the kids understood the way they should lead the life. Everything seemed smooth until one day, when Ardhendu found Anurati weeping under a banyan tree, near her school. She was alone that day. Lisa was absent as she was unwell. He immediately got off his Ranger bike and threw it aside, without bothering to make it stand properly.

"Anu, what happened?" he softly cupped her jaws and lifted her head. Her face was wet with tears and sweat. The moment he touched her warm face, an electrifying effect jerked him. Still with a firm voice, he tried consoling Anurati, who was still shedding tears without telling him what had happened. Ardhendu didn't touch her, since he had dreamed of her a few years ago. But now, he was so close to her that it made him feel awkward. He was distracted. "What if I press her…? What if I kiss her?" He was so distracted that he could not even listen to what Anurati was saying. Unmindfully, he kept asking what made her cry.

"Stop wiping my tears and just leave," frantically Anurati shouted at him.

"Why? What is wrong with you?" he asked, trying to help her stand.

"You are hurting me! Let me make it clear, nothing is wrong with me. It is you who is holding me so hard and is not even realizing what you are saying."

"Oh my god I didn't really mean to do this!" Ardhendu apologized and stepped back and started walking with his hands inside his trouser pockets. Anurati recalled the same picture of Ardhendu when they were discussing Mohanty Sir's acts. She tried changing the topic." Okay, Aru, tell me why are you hanging this camera on to your neck? Want to show that you have one?"

Click! Click! Click!

"Come on don't waste your roll on me!"

"Hey, look. I am not wasting any roll. This is a digital camera. My father got it for me. Click and upload to PC, as many photos as you can!"

"Show me, show me! Wow! New camera, give me a treat?" Anurati touched the camera that was still hanging around his neck. Ardhendu was scared that she might touch her body. He jerked backwards the moment she touched the gadget.

"Let's have ice-cream at the parlour just outside my college gate. Is it fine with you?" he asked.

"Ice-cream, are you mad? Look at the weather!"

"Why? What is wrong with the weather? It is winter, yes, but ice-cream tastes awesome in winter! I always eat it. Today, you try it with me, I bet you will get sharp brains like me," teased Ardhendu. For a moment, everything seemed normal to Anurati. She was scared of bringing up the topic before Ardhendu. She thanked god that he forgot instantly, about why he had stopped by her. She guessed that something was wrong with him. He didn't behave normally as other boys around her did. Now that she said everything, she realized that Ardhendu didn't listen to a single word as he was mentally absent! She was sure that there was some problem in his brain. On the other hand, Ardhendu was embarrassed at the way he behaved with her, so to patch up the relationship he made plans for an ice-cream treat. With two cups of ice-cream, they sat facing each other. Ardhendu asked, "Tell me Anu, why were you crying? Please don't change the topic," he said before she could even interrupt.

"Actually, you know how girls are treated? As if we are sparkling dazzling showpieces! Whoever wants will brush his hand and take advantage of touching it! Okay, one minute, why are you interested in my life?"

"Come on, speak!" Ardhendu adamantly wanted to listen to her feelings. The ice-cream parlour was empty except for these two and the waiter, who was busy watching an old Hindi movie on the television set which was hanging high up from the ceiling. The volume was such that it was audible to both of them. There was silence between them still they could hear the song,

"*Kitaben bahut si padhi hongi tumne, magar koi chehra bhi tumne padha hai...*" (You must have read lots of books but have you ever read a face, romantic song from *Bazigaar*).

Anurati was listening to the song, to avoid the topic. But there was no way could she do this. She was arrested by the way Ardhendu behaved with her. Her heart said, "He is the one who can protect you all your life." But her brain said, "Stay away from this psycho." Actually, it was not her fault. It is our mindset that trouble with a person's brain is termed as 'Madness.' A viewpoint to judge that person's activities changes in every way. Anurati was no different.

"I am waiting. Will you speak?" he asked.

"Oh Aru, I am really scared of this society. I have grown up. I mean to say we have all grown up. Now look at yourself. Your sharp jaw lines, your masculine profile, your voice – you are handsome."

"Thanks for your compliment," shied Ardhendu. No one ever had said such sweet words to him. He was blushing.

"But you know what I have grown with? These attractive, bulging..." Anurati shut her mouth while her hands pointed towards her chest.

"Huh, leave it Aru, let's go," Anurati began moving out of her chair while she was forced by him to sit back.

"Tell me, did something weird happen again?"

"I don't know where to start..." Before she could complete her sentence, Ardhendu interfered saying, "I'm begging you, please." His voice was rude and stern.

"You praise that Muktananda, our chemistry teacher, but you don't know how he behaves with girls. That sicko asks for a pen, and while taking it, he never misses a chance to rub and twist our fingers. Sometimes I feel like hitting him between his legs."

"That lean and thin man does such cheap things! I used to respect him because he was our teacher. But I won't spare him for doing such cheap acts. Why don't you hit him?"

"Forget about this, do you remember I went for my younger cousin's thread ceremony? There, my cousin..."

"Who are you talking about? What is his name?" Ardhendu interrupted.

"Radhav *Bhai*," Anurati shouted loudly. "I must say, Radhav. To hell with *Bhai*! He took a little girl inside a room, a little girl, you understand? Just six-years-old."

"Then?" Ardhendu asked curiously.

"He started undressing her by sliding the frock strap off her shoulder. That little girl didn't even know what this rascal was doing. He started caressing her nipples. I was peeping from the door and barged inside when I saw this and asked him that what he was up to. He fumbled and could not say a single word. I was so furious at that time, I would have killed him, I would have done that!"

"Rascal Radhav."

"You won't even believe it. Radhav is my older paternal aunt's son and Puspi, is my younger paternal aunt's daughter. Someway they are siblings!"

"But I must say – well done on your part. That's what we should do," Ardhendu clapped for her. Anurati continued, ignoring him. "That same night, do you know what happened?"

"Radhav misbehaved with you?"

"No way! He vanished from the place, as I heard later, from the elders."

"So what happened then?"

"That night, Puspi's father, Dinakar *Fufa Ji*..."

"Oh, Dinakar uncle, who usually comes and plays with us?" asked Ardhendu excitedly.

"Yes, that Dinakar uncle," Anurati turned her face and started staring out of the window.

"Hey, what's up?" Ardhendu waved his hands in front of her eyes.

"That sicko, you know... I mean, how do I tell you?" Anurati bit her lips.

"You can tell me. Just speak up. Did he...?" Anurati interrupted him before he could say something. "It was a dimly lit room. I was relaxing in a couch. The television was on. I was awake, but my eyes were closed, and I was thinking about school, classes... then I could see Dinakar standing in front of me, looking here and there, and gradually he came near me. As soon as he reached near my body, my legs almost touching his thighs, he pulled down his trousers and tried making a body part of his touch my leg."

"What nonsense!" Ardhendu was outraged.

"That is why I didn't speak about this to anyone. Not even to my mother. I know you won't believe it. You all think I am making up these stories, and moreover, you might wonder why this is always happening to me!"

"What happened next?" Ardhendu asked.

"Luckily someone called his name and he pulled his trousers up and went away."

"Did he know that you were awake?"

"I don't think so. The next morning, he came with us and we dropped him at the railway station. He was behaving normally, so I think he must not be aware that I saw him."

"Okay, but next time, don't let him do this. He usually visits your house, so be alert."

"Hmmm," Anurati was silent.

"Take it easy; nothing will ever happen to you."

"Why is everyone so attracted towards girls? They are even not scared of doing such things? This problem is even not age specific! It is gender specific, I must say. Males are attracted to young girls! Leave it. This all will simply trouble you. Come on, let us move. It's late." Anurati stood up and so did Ardhendu.

There was complete silence until they reached the main gates and waved each other goodbye. That night, Ardhendu felt helpless. Anurati's incidents were a shock to him. He felt like killing those sick people and wiping them out of society. The effect of this touch was growing within him. He was unable to comprehend why someone was touching a female body without mutual consent. Psychologically, he was disturbed. Now, the effects were outside his body as well. He started trembling and his palms were sweaty. Anurati was the girl he loved dearly, but was worried about her safety. The way society was handling her was not acceptable! He was helpless. The only thing he did was to sit and listen to what had happened to her. He was sad about what was going on around him. Now that his fear was intense, he started visualizing events from the past. He made up his own stories. He wondered if Rout Uncle had torn her shirt. He would have rescued Anurati! He would have covered her naked body with his shoulders around her, and hugged her without hurting her. He rubbed his palms as if rubbing Anurati's naked back. His imagination went wild. However, deep inside, he was scared to be touched by anyone, especially Anurati. Girls should be respected in every way! They should not be treated the way Anurati was treated. Ardhendu and Anurati shared a close bond. Nobody knew that Anurati and Ardhendu were so close. Anurati was happy with what she was doing, and Ardhendu was busy in his own world. They spoke less with each other, when they were with other friends. Aniket was a good friend of Ardhendu's, and her brother, so he never had a doubt on their relationship. He had both trust and respect for both his sister and his dear friend. Now that his fear of touch was intense, he used to sweat even at the thought of being touched by someone. He began staying away from people. He maintained a safe distance from the opposite sex. With Anurati it was very difficult for him to even go close to her and ask her for something. Anurati noticed this, and thought of asking him about it someday.

"He is shy but he is behaving differently now days. I must talk to him soon!" murmured Anurati, watching Ardhendu getting inside the college campus.

CHAPTER SEVEN

Edison, New Jersey. December 2014

One morning, Ardhendu was cheerful. Days were flying. The baby had started kicking, and had started responding to voice. These were very memorable and emotional moments for them. He had never felt this happiness before in life. He was thankful to Anurati. They knew that they were going to have a baby girl. They started shopping for the new member of their family. A cosy room was allotted to the little one and every weekend was dedicated to her. Together, they did a lot of shopping and then back at home, they spent time arranging things. Ardhendu and Anurati would decorate the room. Almost everything was bought - from the pram to a rocker, bibs to booties, from pillows to stuffed kittens. The room looked like a castle, waiting for the arrival of the little princess. The sight of the room made both of them very excited and happy. Anurati was scared of her hidden past. No matter how much she laughed, the back of her mind wondered, 'What if the truth comes out to Ardhendu?' MG! MG! MG! This name echoed in her brain. MG was not dead. However, what will Ardhendu's reaction be, if he found out that MG was still alive? These thoughts never let Anurati's brain rest in peace. After a long time, Ardhendu saw Anurati struggling to wear a sari. He kneeled in front of her and helped her with the pleats.

"Hey you look sexy today..."

"Shut up!" Before he could finish his flirting, he was interrupted.

"Stop staring at me, do the pleats, fast."

"Oh sure, madam! Almost done!" Raising his eyebrows, he finished folding pleats and Anurati stuck a little portion of the folded pleat into her petticoat just above her belly button.

"Thank you, honey," winked Anurati and rushed to the kitchen.

"Slowly, slowly..." Ardhendu prompted from inside the bedroom.

"What is so special today?" he murmured. Faint music from downstairs sounded into his ears. It was in *Odia*. "*Nua arua chaula baati, lekhi de lakhmi pada jhoti*" (Make a semi liquid paste out of soaked new rice grains and put footprints of Goddess *Laxmi,* Hindu goddess of wealth, fortune and prosperity).

"Okay, so *Manabasa Gurubar!*" He noted that it was the Thursday of the ninth month, 'Margasira Masam' in the Hindu calendar. It was *Laxmi puja*! Ardhendu never knew about the rituals that had to be done while worshiping Goddess *Laxmi*. But he ate the *Monda Pitha* which Anurati's mother used to make and send for him. He loved the yummy dim sums! Ardhendu ran downstairs, thinking of those yummy and mouth watering *Mondas*. It was long since he had tasted them. Anurati was pregnant but food craving had caught hold of Ardhendu.

"Stop! Don't touch anything now, please," Anurati shouted at the sight of Ardhendu inside the kitchen.

"But it is so strenuous, let me help you, my baby," pleaded Ardhendu.

"Okay, if you really want me to help, please take a bath and then get inside the kitchen. I am preparing *Prasad,* so go now go and yes, make it fast, please. I really need your help. I am tired."

"At your service, sweetheart. Just give me ten minutes," Ardhendu rushed out.

It was quite early in the morning and too early to take a bath. It was an auspicious day. Anurati was all set to start her *Brata,* the sacred thread which married Odia ladies tie on their upper arm, this year. All married *Odia* ladies were eligible to do this. They took a bath early in the mornings, and according to the *Laxmi Puran,* or the holy book written by Shri Balaram Das in the 15th Century, which raises voices against the evil practices of untouchability in society, and also stresses on the importance of feminism, and empowers the female power to resist the male hegemony, they perform all the rituals, wear new saris, put footprints of *Goddess Laxmi in the* puja room, kitchen, front of closets, bedroom and almost everywhere, to welcome *Mata Laxmi* and to get good fortune. After setting all these things in place, the ladies read the *Puran* and accordingly, tie a thread dipped in turmeric with ten knots in it, each knot depicting a name of *Goddess Laxmi,* in their upper arm. This is called the '*Laxmi Brata.*'

Anurati did exactly what was written in the book. Ardhendu was super excited to watch his pregnant wife doing so many things for him and for his well being. He respected Anurati's devotion for this. At the same time, he was overwhelmed to find how dedicated Anurati was towards all the work she did. He was so proud of her! Soon, they finished their worship and Anurati tied her sacred thread. Now, she kneeled in front of the deity to take a bow, and struggled, but could not, because of her tummy. Then, she tried bowing at Ardhendu's feet, but Ardhendu caught hold of her shoulders and hugged her, saying, "You belong to my heart, so don't you ever try to touch my feet. I hold my breaths for you, my darling!" The only thing he didn't say this time was "I love you." But Anurati said it and completed the scene.

"I must say, you look stunning in a sari!" Ardhendu said, gazing at Anurati. She was slowly taking off the long piece of cloth after a long and busy day with so many rounds of rituals till noon.

"Thank you, but with my bulging stomach, it was very difficult to tie the knot of the petticoat to hold this long and heavy sari!" Anurati took off the sari while saying so. Ardhendu kept staring with his mouth wide open. After a long time, he saw Anurati in a petticoat and blouse, now with her bulging fair-skinned belly. He just went near Anurati and stood behind her. "Aru…" whispered Anurati. But before she could say anything, he caught hold of her tummy from behind. He stroked her red mark by force, pulling down her petticoat a little. Both their eyes met in the mirror. Anurati's cheeks turned pink, complimenting her fair skin. She was literally blushing with Ardhendu's romantic gestures. "You wear the sari after your delivery. Don't hurt yourself! I can't see you in pain," Ardhendu caressed her bare stomach just below her belly button and he dug his middle finger into her belly button which was now wide and big. Gradually, he brushed his palm over her blouse, along the shape of her natural oversized breast. They were tight and firm inside the perfect fitting cotton blouse. However, Anurati stopped him from doing so and smiled at him. They were aware of not moving beyond touching and stroking each other at this stage of pregnancy. But neither of them regretted the current situation. Ardhendu kissed her tummy and said, "Hey, princess what's up? I love you and your mamma too."

"I love you too, *Dadda*!" said Anurati, in a whisper, as if it was the baby saying so. Ardhendu helped Anurati do the rest of her work as she was tired after the morning routine. These days, he was working from home and was grateful for this concept, followed very honestly in America, and he was doing his part perfectly without misusing it. Ardhendu was busy with his *second wife,* his office laptop, as Anurati called it. Anurati, after being physically touched by Ardhendu, was emotionally touched inside her heart. She realized how deeply he loved her. Any details of Mahatab would break his heart, or might break him completely. What should she do to protect her relationship? What should she do to protect Ardhendu? She couldn't push him back to the place where he was suffering from his illness. How terrible was his behaviour earlier? He didn't even let her touch him! He was so scared of touch. Now that he was fine, he touched her gently, kissed her and even caressed her so romantically. Anurati was happy, but at the same time, she was worried about the truth, which was hidden from Ardhendu. Lisa disclosed about Mahatab who was in the same state, but no idea in which city.

"I should not be stressed and yes, I should not lie to Ardhendu either." Anurati spoke to herself. She was determined that she was going to disclose the truth to Ardhendu soon. She decided to write down every piece of information and would ask him to read it, while she would sit beside him, holding his hand and make him understand why she had hidden this from him for so long! She didn't want her husband to get into the trap of the phobia again. These thoughts made her smile. Ardhendu was happy but the work pressure sucked the energy out of him. He leaned back in his chair and closed his eyes as if taking a short nap. But he was awake and was thinking about his past. "Hey darling, tired?" Anurati asked Ardhendu, while stroking his forehead with her hand. "Hmmm," Ardhendu responded almost in a whisper.

"It's almost ten. Come to the bed. Shut down your system, please…" she begged.

"Okay, okay… coming!" he signalled with his, gesturing that he wanted five minutes. He wrapped up everything and was soon in bed inside the comforter. "I forgot one thing; please can you get me the lotion? It is in my pill box!" she asked. "Order me Anu. No need to request something. Your order is my command." Ardhendu went to the dresser, opened the drawer and opened the pill box. But he could not find what he was asked to. "That square pink coloured one," she shouted from inside the comforter.

"*Lacto calamine?*"

"Yes, thank you and please switch off the lights."

"I will do that but you first finish what you are up to," replied Ardhendu.

"No issues dear. You just switch off the lights. I can apply it. It's nothing serious. I need to apply it on my itchy tummy. If I scratch it, I will get stretch marks!" she tried convincing her stubborn husband who was not willing to turn off the light. She had to lift her night gown and apply the lotion to her tummy. She wasn't wearing her leggings under her gown. She was ashamed of lifting her gown, even if it was before her husband. Anurati was bold enough while having sex with Ardhendu, where they both helped each other get naked, but there were still a few things which she didn't want him to watch her do. They had both bathed together, but she closed the washroom door while peeing. She had been naked several hundred times in front of him, but till date, she turned around while changing clothes. Whenever Ardhendu said there was nothing to be hidden from him, he got a neat reply from her – 'She isn't shameless like him' and they both tease each other.

"Come on – give it to me, let me apply it for you."

"No, that's okay, I will do it myself."

"I know – you aren't shameless," Ardhendu came closer to her and kissed her on her forehead. He kept looking deep into her eyes, arresting her completely, and started lifting her gown slowly, upwards. He caught hold of her right arm firmly and strongly, conveying signals to Anurati to let him do what he wanted to. She sighed and clenched her left arm to the bedspread and rubbed both her feet. For a moment, Ardhendu glanced at his pregnant wife, who was lying half-naked in a nude colour panty. He then stroked gently to her fair-skinned thighs, between her legs and then bent down, and kissed her large sized belly button. He could see the stretch marks as bright as her skin, shinning and dazzling. "Anu, Anu…what happened?" Ardhendu broke the silence.

Anurati closed her eyes and nodded her head as if saying, 'No, I can't…I won't.'

"You look so strange. I mean you look so different. I feel, I must also get some experience of pregnancy though I cannot hold the baby inside me, but that's okay. But I feel a father should also get a look at how a mother's body changes during delivery." Ardhendu was very excited to see a pregnant half-naked body. But the excitement was not male arousal though. "Come on Anu, share my feelings. I feel delighted." Ardhendu said, but Anurati didn't look at him. She was feeling very shy about what Ardhendu was doing to her. "Okay, if you truly love me…" before Ardhendu could complete his sentence Anurati turned her head towards him and met his eyes, and nodded, as if saying, "No need of asking whether I love you or not!"

"How do I look?" was the only question she asked.

"You look great. By the way, what made you look so great?" Ardhendu tickled her in her belly button and winked at her.

"You don't know?"

"Un-hu," Ardhendu shook his head.

"Oh, really, then let me tell you. It is you. Your ways of making love! That gave me such a great shape, you rascal," said

Anurati pulling his nose. “Stop looking at me and apply the lotion on my entire tummy!”

“I have never seen a pregnant lady so closely ever. I am sorry – I just said…” before he could confess, Anurati put her palm over his lips and made efforts to take her gown out from her body. “But…” he was again stopped.

“You have every right to see me like this,” Anurati said, lying against her pillows. Now that she had taken off her gown, she was lying with her nude colour underwear only. The colours matched her fair body and it felt as if she was naked. Soon, he applied lotion all over her tummy, slowly and gently.

“Anu, tell me one thing. I have confessed to God, for whatever I did in the past. But I am still scared. What if god takes revenge and hurts our child for my deeds?” Ardhendu spoke softly. He was stroking her tummy.

“Revenge? Hurt? What are you trying to say?”

“I mean – you know, I killed a man and it was intentional! What if god punishes me by…” Ardhendu broke down.

“What? Killed? You saved me! Stop, Aru! Please, please, come near me. You know I can’t reach you. Don’t cry!” Anurati pleaded and pulled him towards her and hugged him stroking his back. “Please calm down. We promised each other that we won’t bring back these topics!” this time Anurati was loud and clear.

“Yeah, I know. We promised. But Anu, I am scared. What if god takes back our life for the life I killed? Every day, I pray for the baby’s long life. Sometimes, I feel like surrendering to the police for killing MG!” She didn’t dare disturb him. She thought if she told him about MG now, it would be difficult for him to comprehend things and he would get a messy picture of what had happened in the past. She thought it was better if he spoke out his mind and relaxed.

"MG?" Anurati reacted as if she was not able to remember the name.

"Mahatab Guru, I know you don't forget things. You remember the incident, but you are trying to calm me down without saying a word on the topic and I think, you are right."

"That's true. Our Angel is listening to what we are speaking. So isn't it good to be quiet and forget what has happened. You didn't kill anyone. Believe me!" Anurati spoke her mind.

"You saw me killing him. Don't you remember?" Ardhendu was loud this time.

"You didn't kill MG. Together, we killed your phobia. Now see – you are fit and healthy!" Anurati tried convincing him that MG was alive and leading a normal life with a lovely wife.

"How can you take things so lightly? The matter is really bad! I killed Mahatab and because I was insane, a psycho – whom people usually tag as mental – I killed a man. I am a murderer!" Ardhendu was literally shouting at Anurati and was standing out of bed, opposite her. For a moment, Anurati felt embarrassed being half-naked, as Ardhendu was fully dressed in his pyjamas. She tried reaching for her night gown, but before she could reach it, Ardhendu caught hold of it.

"Anu, I am sorry. I didn't mean to hurt you. I just said what I always feel," Ardhendu was on his knees. He kept his head on her lap and stopped her from standing up. She stroked his hair and was silent, as she was confused now. She could feel the pain he was living with. Mahatab's death cured his haphephobia but had sowed seeds of guilt all over his body. For an instant, Anu felt like saying, "Aru, you know MG is not dead. He is alive and he is in NJ now!" But she could not say a single word, as this might create misunderstanding on why she had hidden this from him for so many years. She closed her eyes and tears fell on to her naked thighs and rolled to Ardhendu's cheeks.

"No Anu, please don't cry. I can't forgive myself if you shed tears. You know I get furious and shout when I get angry. My brains don't listen to my heart – the place where you stay," he instantly got up and wiped her tears, putting her left palm on his chest.

"No, I am not crying," said Anurati, rubbing the back of her right palm over her pinkish chubby cheeks.

"Whatever I am today is because of you. You are everything to me and I owe every single breath to you. I was a mad man as people tagged me but you stepped forward, sacrificed everything and made the person I am today," Ardhendu broke down again.

"No, not again, please Aru," this time it was mischievous. Anurati put her palms over her ears and shouted at top of her voice in order to calm him down. Ardhendu stopped at once and was shocked to see how his wife was behaving. She was like a four-year-old! "Yeah, yeah – you owe your life to me, so do you really want me to take it back, *Mishra Ji*?" Anurati was unmindfully standing half-naked with her both hands in her hips. With this tensed atmosphere, she had actually forgotten that she was half-nude.

"Wait a second," Ardhendu came near her and touched her wet bra asking, "Is she sweating?"

"No, fool. You are a science student, right?" said Anurati, slapping his palm over her breast.

"Yeah, but I didn't read so much in detail about pregnant ladies."

"Okay, stop. I am lactating. Nothing to worry," said Anurati turning her back to him. She took out her breast from the cup of her bra and patted it dry with a Turkish towel. She then took out a camisole, pulled the night gown from the bed and headed straight to the washroom. This time, she wasn't stopped by Ardhendu. Ardhendu was actually unsure of the bodily changes she was going through. But he thought of educating himself. Anurati thanked god for her lactating breast. She wasn't prepared to disclose the matter of MG, but she was just about to. She cleaned herself and dressed up properly, came and lay down in her bed. Without even bothering about Ardhendu, she simply wished him goodnight and made herself comfortable under the comforter. It was the end of December and it was freezing outside. Though the centralized room heater made life normal inside, she felt cold, as she lay under the comforter. She smiled to herself at the thought of standing in a two-piece, just a few minutes ago.

"Ardhendu is such a darling," she whispered to herself and fell asleep. Ardhendu did his research on pregnant women. He saw some videos on YouTube, yawned about fifteen or twenty times before finally coming back to his wife, when he saw her asleep.

"Yes, she is tired. My darling, goodnight," he whispered in her ear and kissed her forehead and snuggled under the comforter. "I should not have told her about MG. He is her past. He is dead. What is her fault in this?" Ardhendu kept talking to himself. He even said, "She is great. She married me after knowing everything. She hasn't ever questioned me about my illness. Her love for me is so selfless and more than that 'I love her.'"

CHAPTER EIGHT

Rourkela, Odisha; February, 2002

"Hi Aunty!" Anurati waved at Kamli Aunty, her neighbour, who was having tea and snacks with Anurati's mother.

"Hello, Anu how was your day? Your daughter has grown so beautiful, Mrs. Acharya!"

"Thank you," Anurati's proud mother smiled broadly. The very next minute, she asked about her biological development and growth which both women shared secretly in whispers. Anurati could guess from her room that these ladies were talking about periods and bra sizes. She just ignored everything and concentrated on her work. They had an early dinner. It was just 8:30 PM when they ate.

"Anu, after you have your food, go to Kamli Aunty's house," Anurati's mother said, munching her piece of *Chapati.*

"Sure mamma, do you want me to bring you something from her?" Anurati asked unmindfully, reading her '*H C Verma*' Physic book.

"No, go and stay with her for the night."

"What?" Both Aniket and Anurati responded.

"Not you, Aniket, only Anu."

"But why? She can sleep alone. She does that every time! Uncle always stays away! I cannot go every night," Anurati stopped reading and was surprised at what her mother said.

"While leaving, Kamli asked me to send you as she is scared to sleep alone. You will have a good time, Anu. I promised her," Anurati's mother said.

"But mamma, I don't feel like going to her house alone. Can Aniket come with me?"

"No, no. It won't be nice. Aniket is a big boy now. Try to understand these things," Anurati's mother said as she began cleaning the mess from the dining table. Anurati's father and Aniket had already left the table and were busy watching TV. "Kamli Aunty is nice. You will have nice a time together. Don't sleep late! You have school tomorrow. Get up early!"

"Bye daddy, bye bro," said Anurati, as she left to Kamli Aunty's place.

"Listen, Anu," her mother called.

"Yes, mamma?" she replied, turning around at the front door.

"You didn't change into your night dress? You won't be comfortable. So change and go."

"No, it won't look good. It's okay. I will manage in my T-shirt and Capris. Don't worry mamma!" She waved goodbye and left. Her mother watched her entering the gates and then go in through Kamli's doorway. She relaxed.

"Pretty girl!" Aunty said as Anurati entered the house.

Anurati sighed in her mind and said, "Thank you, Aunty."

"You had dinner?"

"Yes Aunty, all done. I have a Physics test. So you sleep. I will read and sleep late."

Kamli Aunty asked Anurati to follow her to the bedroom where she could read. When she finished, she could sleep.

Kamli Aunty took out her books so that she could stay busy while Anurati studied. Kamli Aunty lay down in her bed. She was younger than Anurati's mother. She was in her late twenties, a very smart and beautiful lady. Two years' ago, she married Mr Saxena, who was posted in the Indian Navy. It was due to his job that she was left alone for many days at a time. She seemed happy and content, though. Anurati was too young to understand the loneliness of a wife. But she was matured enough to understand attraction. Kamli Aunty's body was perfect. She wore a satin nightgown which almost clung to every curve of her body. It wasn't transparent, but the yellow colour complimented her brown skin. It was enough for someone to gaze at her, with a mouth wide open.

"Hey Anu, what are you staring at?" Aunty asked Anurati.

"Nah, Aunty, nothing I was just seeing…" before she could say something, Aunty asked, "My body or my curves?"

"What?" Anurati was puzzled and embarrassed. But she was staring at her curves. Aunty was right. She took out her Physics book and started reading.

"I was just kidding, Anu. You are a grownup girl. You are even mature enough to be teased. Isn't it?"

"Of course! I am eighteen!" she said proudly.

"Ohho! Eighteen! No more a minor? Eligible for *everything*," Aunty teased and tickled Anurati.

Anurati giggled and started reading her Physics book. She was studious. Kamli Aunty took out a few books and picked out one to read. She fell asleep, soon. After Anurati finished her required lessons, she caught hold of a book lying near Aunty. She thought of stacking them back so that they wouldn't hurt Aunty if she turned in her sleep. However, she was shocked to see the cover pages of the three books that were upside down. The heading was "Bestseller, Porn." All the three books had images of naked men and women – kissing, hugging and touching each other. Anurati realized that she was breathing very hard. She was seeing these pictures for the first time. She could not refrain from seeing them. Her age and eagerness made her peep into the books for a few hours into the night. She scanned every page and finally fell asleep. Before she could get up in the morning, it was Aunty who stroked her forehead and asked her to wake up, lest she be late for school.

"Oh Aunty! Good morning!" Anurati wished her, rubbing her sleepy eyes.

"Good morning, Anu! Your mamma asked me to send you soon."

"Oh my god! 7:30! I have to rush Aunty. See you!" Anurati got up from bed and ran. She heard Aunty say, "See you in the evening!" She responded in the affirmative. That evening Anurati finished her homework, dinner and told her mother that she was leaving for Aunty's place. Her mother seemed happy that Anurati didn't complain about going to Kamli's place, but she was unaware of what made Anurati so excited to go.

"You don't have your books today?" Aunty asked as soon as Anurati entered her house.

"No, the test is over. I did my best, as usual. Next test will be next week. So relax!" Anurati kept talking about her classes, school, friends and teachers. Aunty was listening to her raptly. She was alone all day, just watching television. She was happy about it – and enjoyed the company. However, at the same time, she had a craving for sex. She was plotting in her mind to fulfil her desire with Anurati. But she could not judge whether Anurati would let her do something like that or if she would oppose her, and because of that, she didn't dare to touch her. She was happy with just her presence. She thought of exposing Anurati to the world of sex, but slowly and gradually. She knew that being eighteen, her hormones would definitely get excited. It was because of her these desires, that she was thrown out of her in-laws' house. But it was all just gossip, as nobody was an eye – witness to it. It was in her crooked brain. She had made plans of being physical with a young girl like Anurati. While watching TV, Anurati called for Kamli Aunty and went to the kitchen.

"Yes Anu? I am here in the bedroom, changing my sari!" she shouted from inside the bedroom. She thought Anurati might come inside. So she threw her sari away and stood facing the door, in her petticoat and blouse.

"Okay you carry on. I just wanted a drink of water."

Burning with desire, Kamli tore her blouse with force. The buttons flew and fell on ground. She was in a mood to walk in front of Anurati with only her petticoat and bra on. But she somehow managed and controlled herself. She put on a see-through nightgown in cream. It was a two-piece floral nightgown and was very elegant. The moment Anurati saw Aunty in her nightgown, she jumped up to her feet and came to her.

"Wow! Aunty! You look so HOT!" She sent a few flying kisses her way and went back to watching television. Transparency didn't matter. She didn't even look beyond Aunty's face.

"Anu, switch off the TV. Your mother would scold me if you are awake till late!" Aunty ordered furiously. Her voice made Anurati obey rather than argue, as she used to do with her mother back at home. Anurati picked up a rectangular piece of paper and read aloud the message on it, "I SHALL BE BACK HOME SWEETHEART STOP."

"Is this a telegram? Uncle will be back home, Aunty?"

"Yeah, your uncle will be back tonight."

"So you must be happy! But you could have told me not to come!" Anurati was surprised. Aunty was now lying on her bed with her sleeveless gown. She had taken off her netted overcoat.

"You didn't finish your books yesterday? Am I not correct?" Aunty asked Anurati mischievously

"Which books Aunty?" She didn't want to discuss that she had seen those books, so she blankly looked at her and licked her dry lips with her wet tongue.

"Don't worry. I am not going to tell your mamma. It will be a secret between you and me. I promise!"

"I am sorry. I read your story…" Before she could complete her sentence, Aunty threw the books in front of her, leaving the cover side up for her. Anurati was ashamed of what she saw, but Aunty freely talked about those pictures and tried educating her. Anurati was dumbstruck. There was a long silence between the two. Only Aunty kept turning the pages one by one, and was enjoying the book with Anurati. Anurati felt a wetness rise between her legs, but she didn't exactly know what was happening to her. Kamli Aunty closed all books and asked her to sleep as she might wind up getting late in the morning. Anurati slept, but was luckily not touched by Aunty.

"Shhh! Please don't make noise," Kamli said in a hissing voice.

With this hissing sound Anu opened her eyes and was awake. It was too dark to recognize who else was in bed. She could feel the presence of a third person with Aunty. She could feel the motion of her bed – it was moving as if she was travelling in a train. But she didn't dare to wake up. What would she see in front of her? There might be two naked bodies! She pretended as if she was sleeping and let them settle down.

"I missed you so much," Kamli whispered near the ear of the dark shadow which Anurati could see from the streetlights shining in through the window pane. Anurati could feel the nightgown over her arms. She was now fully awake. A live telecast of cricket is mind-blowing! But this was more than that for her.

"I would have been wild. Only because of you, I am gentle. We should have moved to the other room. A big girl is sleeping near you. What if she gets up Kamli?" asked a husky male voice.

"Darling, she is a big girl. She won't get up," said Kamli by pressing her right palm on Anurati's palm. Anurati didn't know how to respond to what Kamli Aunty did. So she pressed back her palms in return and bit her tongue between her teeth in that gloomy scary night.

"Listen *Janu,* I am with my husband, in my bedroom. So neither am I scared nor ashamed of. Is that clear?" this time her tone was quite loud and clear.

"Okay, okay, now shut up and don't be loud," Mr. Saxena whispered.

From the black night to the silvery dawn, the time was too long for Anurati. The night was the longest night ever for her. In the middle of the night, she thought of using the washroom, but out of fear, she stayed put in one position all night. She stayed put until Aunty asked her to get up and leave. Without looking at her, she rushed home. But out of the corner of her eye, she saw Aunty in a sari and uncle fast asleep on the sofa in the living room. She thought it was a bad dream. The incident that happened the night before moved her life. She thought that the two-night stay at Kamli Aunty's place was a nightmare.

Anurati thanked god that uncle was back, and that he would stay for at least six months. After six months, she wouldn't be there, so no more nights to spend with that dangerous lady! Anurati was aware that Aunty knew that she was awake the whole night. She saw two bodies moving, up and down, right and left. It was dark, but any sensible person can sense what the two adults were busy doing, wrapping and unwrapping themselves in the sheets all night. Anurati was no longer a kid. Dark shadows really made deep imprints in Anurati's heart and mind. Though nobody messed with her, she was exposed to a kind of cruelty - the act took place in front of her eyes and that was not anything less than a sinful offence.

Anurati was restless all day. She sat alone on a bench in the park. She tried erasing every dirty image from her mind and tried forgetting everything. She rubbed her left palm hard with her right palm, as if omitting the previous night's touch. She could not comprehend why that lady did such a thing!

"Whoa," a noise from behind the park bench scared her. Anurati didn't react to what Ardhendu said. She simply stared at him.

"No reaction. Are you alright?"

"I am fine."

"But I don't think so."

"What do you mean?" Anurati raised her voice unmindfully.

"Your eyes speak a lot to me. You can't hide anything from me," Ardhendu spoke confidently.

"Let's not sit here. It's a park. People will start talking about you and me! Come on, let's move!" She said and started walking towards her cycle. This time, she decided not to share anything with Ardhendu. What could she say to Ardhendu, and about what? The pornographic books and the nude pictures? Or the insane couple who didn't even seek privacy during their most intimate moments? She thought she could say nothing of these ever, to anybody. She walked hurriedly and unlocked her bicycle. But before she could pedal away, Ardhendu caught hold of her hand. The moment he touched her arm, his palms started trembling and sweat accumulated, but he was concerned about Anurati.

"I heard you were with that Kamli for last two nights?" It was a question rather than a statement, direct and to the point.

"Yes… so?" Anurati fumbled for a while but later stared rudely as if saying, "It's my life – let me live it my way."

"No, nothing. I just heard from Aniket and was worried for you!"

"But why are you worried about me? It was my mother who asked me to go to her place. I had no choice and thought of…" but before Anurati could complete her sentence Ardhendu interrupted saying something very true.

"Anu, Kamli is not a good company to be with. Stay away from her. She is honey-dipped poison." For a while Anurati was stunned. She wondered how come he knew so much about Kamli. Was he…? Ardhendu could read her mind so before she could complete her thoughts he said, "You know Rout Uncle and Kamli Aunty…together …how do I explain to you?" Ardhendu fumbled for words.

"You mean – affair?"

"Beyond that, they are not the Romeo-Juliet type." The word '*Beyond*' was quite clear to Anurati now. She thought they must have done that stupid thing together, that Kamli is a witch and that Rout Uncle a monster.

"Why are you silent? You don't believe me?"

"I trust you. I would not have, but the two nights I spent, explains everything Aru," Anurati said so without even thinking of what she should say and what she should not.

"Huh, there you are. Tell me, what happened?" he asked.

"Listen Aru, It's true that something happened. But let me make it very clear that I won't tell you. I mean I can't. Not now. Not ever. Is that clear? So let's move. It's getting dark," Anurati sat in her bicycle seat and said so and pedalled away. He couldn't stop her this time.

Ardhendu thought of all wild possibilities of Anurati and Kamli being involved. He even imagined them nude and clinging to each other. This time, his thoughts made him fearful. He started sweating at the thought of Anurati. His pulse raced fast. He could hear his heartbeats and breaths together. His palms were wet with sweat. He was sinking with fear. The fear of touch, the fear of being touched by the opposite sex, be it Anurati – the love of his life, or anyone else. His condition was now devastating. He wondered how he was going to spend the rest of his life. Most of his days passed this way. He was unaware of what was going on with him. He cared only for his studies, his practical work and rarely visited friends. He was very shy with his classmates. Nobody knew about his hidden illness. He limited his social interactions. He didn't interact with girls, except Anurati. It was only a week ago that he had met Anurati. He was scared of meeting her. On the other hand, Anurati was really upset. She could not forgive herself for treating Ardhendu like she did, in the park. She could have been gentle, kind and even polite. She wondered what there was to hide from him. He knew every incident that she didn't even dare to speak to her mother about. There was nothing to hide from him, about that night. She decided she would go over to Ardhendu's place and talk to him about it.

"Anu madam, please come in! Aru *baba* is in his room. Please go inside," said Ardhendu's maid, answering the door and finding Anurati.

Nodding, Anurati went inside. She thought of surprising Ardhendu. Without making a noise, she walked slowly and peeped into Ardhendu's room, whose door was partially open. She froze at the sight of Ardhendu. She could see Ardhendu's bare back with drizzles of sweat reflecting the light. He was busy looking at the screensavers, which seemed to be changing one after the other, every ten seconds. The pictures that came one after the other in his monitor were those of Anurati's. She even heard him saying, "Don't touch me. Why do you let others touch you? Please, stay away! Don't come near me! You scare me. See, my pulse is beating so fast, even if you only look at me!" Anurati was stunned. She could not believe her eyes or her ears. She saw him pulling his hair and punching the wall hard with his fist. This sight frightened Anurati more than anything she had undergone in the past. She was there to surprise him but she was surprised herself at his condition! She didn't dare knock the door. She thought of leaving the place before Ardhendu pounced at her and mistreated her. Earlier, she guessed that he had a problem in his brain but now, she confirmed that Ardhendu was mentally unstable. He was, *a psycho*. She thought he was dangerous and left the place. The surroundings around Anurati disturbed her, but with strong determination, hard work and will power, she did well in her twelfth standard board examinations. She cleared the CET - (Common Entrance Test), for admission into the four years' Bachelor of Physiotherapy course and got a seat in the Nopany Institute of Healthcare Studies, Kolkata. Now, she was all set to leave Rourkela and move into a new life: this time, at a hostel. She decided that she would try to forget the past and the people of the past and start a new life at a new place with her new career in tow. She was excited for all these things happening in her life. She thought of meeting Ardhendu for the last time to bid him goodbye. There was an invisible attraction within her, for him, that always made her think of him.

"Hi! All set for hostel life?" Ardhendu asked Anurati, knocking on the already opened door.

"Oh hi, you are here? Yeah almost done," Anurati asked surprisingly.

"Aniket said you are leaving for Kolkata today evening and you want to meet me."

"Actually my scores in CET…"

"Yeah Anu, I know your whereabouts, your scores, your college, your courses of study and about your hostel. Don't worry, it is a safe place. I asked my Bengali friends."

"It's great that you know everything."

"Don't you want to know how I know so many things about you?"

"From Aniket, of course," she answered.

"Okay, then don't you want to know why I am interested in you?" Anurati remained silent. She visualized Ardhendu before his PC, pulling his hair, punching his fist and growling her name. "Did you hear me?" Ardhendu asked again.

"You are a sweet friend of mine," she smiled. In her mind, she was scared at what his next question would be.

"Anu, I love you," Ardhendu spoke these golden words almost in a whisper. Anurati heard him, but behaved as if she didn't. She groaned and pressed her oversized suitcase to zip it and looked up at Ardhendu for help.

"Little more force and it will close," she kept talking about closing her suitcase and didn't let Ardhendu speak. "Yeah, it's done. Thank you, Aru!"

"Anu, I said I love you." Anurati turned her back to him and gathered courage to say something. "I know I should have got a gift for you. I should have gone down on my knees and should have..." Before he could say anything more, Anurati stopped him. "No, Aru. I don't think this is the proper time. I mean you are a good friend, but I don't think you can..."

"Take it easy Anu. I just thought of expressing my feelings for you. I have loved you for long and I will love you all my life. You have every right to your opinion. It's okay. Good luck."

"Listen, Aru, I trust you more than I trust myself. You know me better than anyone else does. I read those dirty books at Kamli's place and you won't believe that the lady and her husband had sex in the same bed that I was in! I didn't sleep that night and was busy listening to what they were whispering. See how easily I can tell these things to you? You are a very dear friend of mine. I might need you in my life but just let me know honestly, will you be able to support me in every way? Please, don't misunderstand me. Let me live my life and you live yours."

"Let me tell you, I got an offer for a position in an MNC at the campus interview. After the final semester, I shall join their Bangalore office."

"Congrats! However, I didn't mean this *support,* Aru!" Anurati wanted him understand that she meant something else. She wanted to tell him that he was mentally unstable to lead a normal life, to marry a girl and have kids. But she didn't want to end up hurting him, either.

"You are my life and I love you. Take your time. Someday, if you feel your heart is beating for me, then let me know.

I shall wait for your response all my life. Bye for now, Anu." Ardhendu didn't want to force Anurati into this relationship. He waved goodbye and went away without waiting for any other clarification from her. After a few hours, Anurati was on the train, gazing into the darkness outside from her window. There would be a light pole, passing every five seconds in a regular pattern. She had left Rourkela forever. She left a dear friend, Ardhendu - no, not a friend anymore. She left somebody who loved her more than anything else in this world. She had left her home. She had left her parents. She had left her brother. She kept wiping her tears but they flowed faster. After college, she would marry someone and step into his world. All her childhood was a sweet memory which she could only live out in her dreams. In one corner of her heart, she was excited to start her career and lead her independent life. Once she thought of Ardhendu's proposal, she was happy that she gathered courage to deny the psycho's proposal. With all these sad and happy thoughts, she pulled the bed sheet over her head from under her toes. She wasn't alone. Her father was with her, right below in the middle berth. She covered herself completely and slept without any tension about her luggage and baggage.

CHAPTER NINE

Edison, New Jersey. March 2015

Before Anurati had left her bed, Ardhendu was ready for office. "Honey, you didn't wake me up?" asked questioningly.

"You can sleep. It's okay! Some urgent work has come up. I have to rush," he rushed downstairs before she could say anything else. Gobbling up a piece of frozen sandwich and grasping a can of juice, he shouted at the top of his voice, "Take care of yourself and our princess too. I will be back soon." He locked the front door by turning the knob from inside. Anurati struggled to get up from bed as it was almost time for the baby to come, but with the thud of the door, she sank back in her comforter.

"*Kuchi, kuchi...* Dadda didn't kiss you goodbye? It's okay dear! Mamma will do that for dadda and mamma both!" Anurati stroked her palm against her full belly and whispered to her baby.

Outside, Ardhendu turned the key, the car briefly chortled, then began to purr – but stopped. He again turned the key, but once again, the car briefly chortled, began to purr and stopped. Ardhendu tried another five to six times. He was getting late, so he instantly called a garage, gave them the details and rushed out of the car. He then called his colleague and told him to carry on with the meeting, and that he would be late to office. He briefed them about his car's condition. Ardhendu opened the rear door of the car, but his file of reports was missing.

He stood still for a while, counted backwards from ten to one, and then relaxed. Slowly walking over the snow, he went back to the house, opened the front door with his keys and entered inside. Before Anurati was frightened with the sound, he immediately called her name.

"Anu, Anu – It's me, downstairs."

"Huh! Your dadda is still here!" Anurati was puzzled. This time, she struggled hard to get out of the bed. She turned to her side, put her legs down, adjusted her gown over her tummy, back and thighs and put on her slippers then slowly moved out of the room shouting, "Wait, please wait. We are coming."

"Don't rush. I am not leaving. Take your time." Ardhendu collected his file that he had left while wearing his shoes. He waved his file at Anurati, who was coming downstairs, holding her belly protectively, as if she were holding a huge beach ball wrapped in a piece of cloth.

"Okay! You forgot your file? We thought you came back to give us a goodbye kiss!" Anurati chuckled.

"Anu, do you have some change? I have a $20 bill. I might need it in the Metro Park Station."

"You are going by train? Where? Why?"

"The car broke down. The mechanic will come. Just give him the keys. They are in the drawer." Ardhendu said, pointing at the chest of drawers near the shoe rack. "And yes, as soon as the meeting gets over, I shall be back. Don't stress yourself. Lisa is back, so you can call her! You will have company." Ardhendu touched Anurati's tummy as if blowing a flying kiss at the baby and rushed outside without even waiting to listen to what she was saying. Anurati understood him. He must have some important work, as otherwise, he would not have left her alone. She said, "Don't worry. We will both be fine, darling." No one was there to listen, but she was sure that Ardhendu must have heard her say so." See? Your dadda came back to say bye to us. Happy now?" Anurati stroked her tummy and chatted with her baby. This time, she felt a response from within, as if saying, "Yes mamma, dadda is so sweet."

"What? Aru went by train?" she suddenly spoke out loud to herself and sat back, blank, with her mouth and eyes wide open. Her brain started visualizing and thinking of possibilities. What if he met Mahatab in transit? Why the hell did the car break down? Was it that something big was going to happen? All these thoughts made her weak. She fetched a glass of water and quenched her thirst.

Anurati suddenly heard a knock on the front door. She got distracted. Ardhendu never knocked on the door. He always had his set of keys. Slowly, she got off the couch and walked, taking baby steps towards the front door. The knocks grew persistent, and Anurati wondered why the visitor wasn't ringing the doorbell. She looked through the peephole, but couldn't see anyone. Without opening the door, she simply dialled Ardhendu's number from her phone, which she held in her left hand.

"Hello, Aru?"

"Open the door."

"What?" Anurati disconnected the call, threw the phone, which flew like a Frisbee before landing on the couch. "Oh, dear!" Anurati caught hold of Ardhendu's arm. He struggled to stand up on the icy floor. There were frozen pieces of ice – looking like icicles, all over the patio railings. He entered inside. There was heavy snowfall the night before, but the maintenance guy didn't put rock salt over the stairs, so it was still slippery. Ardhendu slipped from the stairs and fell. Luckily, there were not many stairs. However, a fall is a fall. He was wet and dirty. With her help, he came inside.

"Don't worry. I am fine. Oh! My back!" Ardhendu said, walking slowly, holding his back. He started undressing. He took off his shoes first. His socks were dry and fine, he pulled off his trousers. He threw the wet clothes about and told Anurati not to worry. He would put them in the laundry basket, later.

"Show me!" Anurati said, coming beside Ardhendu. She stood behind him. She lifted his shirt and checked, but could not find any sign of bruises. There were a few on his palms.

"Anu, I will get you Moov. Will you please spray it on my back so it relieves the pain?" Ardhendu said, and walked up to a room. He got the spray from the pill box.

"Are you still going to office?" Anurati asked, spraying the pain reliever.

"Thank you so much Anu. I shall go and change."

"I think it is okay if you don't go today."

"No, Anu. I have a lot of work. Otherwise, you know me. First, my car broke down. Now, I broke. I am still struggling to go to office!" In no time, he was back and started wearing another pair of shoes. He glanced at her. She was upset at what was happening all around. "Cheer up Anu. I will be back soon and yes, nothing will happen to me this time."

"First you forgot your file, then your car broke down, and now you got hurt. I am worried, Aru."

"Take it easy. So many things already happened. What else is left? Be happy and let me go," Ardhendu cupped his palms around her chubby cheeks and kissed her on her forehead. He waved goodbye and moved out. Anurati remained silent and thought that these were all signals from the Almighty, to stop

Ardhendu from meeting Mahatab. But she saw the wall clock showing ten. Usually, people start the day early in the US – by 8:00 AM. He was already late by two hours. Then, she thought that maybe Ardhendu was right. So many things had already happened. What else was left? She tried relaxing, but was restless, thanks to her pregnancy. The last days were making her agitated. She had a feeling of taking out the baby from her tummy and lying down flat on her belly, as she used to do before pregnancy. She even thought that having her monthly periods were better than pregnancy. "Ouch!" Anurati got a tight kick on her tummy, which brought her back to where she was sitting grasping her big belly. "I am sorry. I am sorry, my baby! You are angry with mamma? Mamma promises that she will love you more when you come out. Come fast, please. I can't wait any longer!" For the time being, she was distracted.

"Come on, Lisa! Pick up the call," Anurati kept blabbering after dialling Lisa's number. But after a few seconds, she heard the *i*nteractive voice response. She disconnected the call without leaving a message and decided to call back again after some time. Somehow, Ardhendu managed to walk to the Metropark Station. He wasn't a pass holder, so he purchased tickets for the onward and return journeys and entered the train that was on time. He scrutinized his reports page by page. After a few minutes, he heard a recognizable disembodied voice. Ardhendu tried recalling the voice. "Where have I heard this orotund voice? I know this person!" unmindfully, he continued turning his reports page by page. He was distracted with the voice. He heard Lisa's name in between his telephone conversation. He heard the man say, "Okay, fine, Lisa. I shall come home and pick the both of you up. We shall go to New York this Saturday. Bye. See you soon!"

Before Ardhendu could get up and check the man, he walked out fast, through the automatic doors at the stop prior to Ardhendu's. But from his tall physique, the back of his body and most importantly, his unique, orotund voice, Ardhendu could not believe his eyes or ears. He simply sat back, closing his eyes. His mind kept rewinding and showing flashes of whom he saw. "Mahatab? But how is that possible? Is he still alive? But I killed him! He wasn't even breathing! The doctor also declared him dead!" By the time he could analyze his thoughts, the train halted. Unmindfully, he stepped out of the train and was very disturbed. He tried consoling himself. "No, it must be my imagination!" Ardhendu sat on an iron bench in the station and hastily dialled Lisa's number. He could hear the beeping sounds and the call got disconnected. He tried a few more times and finally heard the *IVR* say that his call was waiting. After disconnecting the call, he saw the clock showing the current time. He was very late for his meeting. Without delaying any further, he moved on but was determined to call Lisa later to enquire about her Saturday plans. Here, at home, Anurati was busy narrating the morning's incidents to Lisa and vice versa.

"I have invited Mahatab on Saturday and together we are going to NY."

"What? You are going to meet him? You have even planned a trip to NY?" Anurati shouted at Lisa.

"Why? What happened? You both can join us. Oops! Would-be mommy can't go. Okay, okay! Let's change this to a lunch party. No trips. Now are you happy?"

"Shut up Lisa! You don't know..." Anurati was very serious this time. She wasn't giggling or smiling. Lisa could sense something fishy and interrupted.

"*Jiju* knows Mahatab, right? He was your Ex-" before Lisa could complete her sentence Anurati stopped her.

"He wasn't my ex-boyfriend. I never loved him. But I must say he was a very special person to me who once..."

"Oh special...I mean secret special...once what? Helped you lose your virginity?" Anurati was furious at what she said, but tried relaxing. "Hello? Hello? Are you there Anu?"

"Yes, in a phone call only one person speaks and the other listens. I was on the listening side," Anurati seemed irritated at what Lisa had just said.

"So, your affair went a little further and you aborted his baby and all this is still hidden from *Jiju*, right?"

"What rubbish! Don't you think before you speak?"

"Listen, if you had an affair and now want me to hide from your husband, I can do it but for a price. If ready, then you can trust me as always."

"Just stop blabbering and don't create stories. There is something else beyond this and it is a matter of life and death, which even Aru doesn't know. So don't just talk nonsense, Lisa!"

Like Ardhendu, Lisa was unaware of the incident. She could not imagine what it could be. Finally, Anurati asked Lisa to do something to stop Mahatab from meeting Ardhendu and she promised her to disclose the truth to Ardhendu soon, and even tell her all the secrets related to Mahatab in their next meeting. Before Anurati disconnected the call, she heard Lisa say that she had a missed call from Ardhendu. She was exhausted and was panting. She stretched her leg and lay down on the couch.

In the office, it was a busy day for Ardhendu. He didn't get a chance to interact with Lisa. Only during lunch break he called Anurati.

"Hello!" answered a sleepy voice.

"Hey, you are fine? Did I disturb you?"

"No, it's okay, I was just relaxing but I don't know how I slept for so long," Anurati saw the time and slowly stood up.

"I had my lunch. What about you?"

"Boohoo, I slept for so long and now I am hungry," Anurati said in a very childish way.

"Oh Anu, it's okay. Go grab something from the freezer. Don't starve. I shall be back by evening. Did you call Lisa?"

"Of course, we chatted for an hour."

"That's great. Why don't you ask her to come home this Saturday? The four of us will have lunch together. I shall cook some special dishes and we shall have some fun together. It's been long since we had a get-together."

"But she is going to…I mean she may have some other plans?" Anurati paused, before disclosing Lisa's plans.

"You said she is going somewhere. Where is she going?" Ardhendu asked curiously, rewinding the telephone conversation of that man he had heard, in his mind.

"I don't know, Aru! Listen, we shall have our Saturday lunch. You, me and our baby!" she tried distracting him.

"Okay, let's give her a surprise visit. What do you say?" Ardhendu said adamantly.

"Why? Don't you like spending time with your pregnant wife? What is there in Lisa, that you want to be with her so desperately?" Anurati said, outraged.

"What nonsense! Okay, leave it! I don't want to argue with you anymore on this topic!" Anurati sensed that Ardhendu was upset with what she had told him. This was the only way to stop him from meeting Lisa.

"Waa, waa! You shouted at me," Anurati pretended as if she was crying.

"No, Anu, I am sorry. It's okay. We shall have our lunch on Saturday. Please stop crying."

Anurati stopped her melodrama this time and grabbed a frozen sandwich and put it inside the microwave. She asked Ardhendu to come home early and disconnected the call.

"An *idle mind is a Devil's workshop!*" Anurati could not analyze why Ardhendu was so adamant about going to Lisa's place. He never did that! She was disturbed, with all kinds of thoughts messing up her mind. She even thought that Lisa might have spoken to Ardhendu about Mahatab. She told herself, "Time is the best healer for every solution, so let me give this some time!" She tried calling Lisa, but unfortunately, the call could not be completed. In the office canteen, after disconnecting the call, Ardhendu called Lisa. Luckily, he got connected!

"Hello *Jiju*, how are you? How is your back?" Lisa asked.

"I am a bit better now. I heard you and Anu chatted for long today. Why didn't you come home? Anyway, before that, why don't you and Anshuman join us for lunch on Saturday?" Ardhendu was not convinced with the way Anurati put things. He boldly asked Lisa to find out about her weekend plans.

"Oh! So sweet of you to invite us for lunch! However, sorry we have to decline, we have some other plans!" said Lisa, very carefully, without saying much else. She tried not to let the matter worsen. She was already aware that something was going on between Anurati, Ardhendu and Mahatab.

"What plans? Come on! We shall have fun together. You know her due date is very near. Once the baby comes, no more get-togethers like this!"

"Let me tell you the truth."

"Yes, you should. That will be better," Ardhendu's voice was quite stern and serious. All his laughter vanished.

"Actually, an old friend is coming to visit us. He is here for a seminar and will return to India soon!" Before she could give him any other information, she was fired with questions and she could not even understand why Ardhendu was behaving so differently.

"Old friend? What's his name? Do I know him?"

"No *Jiju*, he is Anshuman's school friend. Okay, I think somebody is at the door. I shall call you back. Bye *Jiju*," Lisa intentionally disconnected the call. She was scared to lie to Ardhendu. She thought that the more she spoke, the more complicated things would become. Ardhendu was sure that something fishy was going on behind his back. The way Lisa hung up had forced him to think so.

"The man I heard and saw is Mahatab!" Ardhendu sat back on the couch in the cafeteria, holding his head in his arms, applying mild force." My eyes and my ears can't lie. He is Mahatab Guru!" his voice was a whisper. He closed his eyes and thought of Anurati and his baby. He thought of the message he once got from Mahatab. "I WILL SLEEP WITH YOUR ANU. SAVE HER VIRGINITY IF U CAN, U SICK IMPOTENT PSYCHO!"

This disturbed him. His thoughts and emotions were waging a war inside him. His mind said, "Whose baby is it?" His heart claimed, "Of course, it is my baby!" For the first time in his life, he thought he was being betrayed by his wife! If she could make a live person dead, it is possible for her to do anything behind his back. He thought of her as selfish and heartless, for playing with other's emotions. "I killed Mahatab. I pressed the pillow and choked him to death. Anu was behind me. The doctor declared him dead and issued a death report citing cardiac arrest as the reason. I wanted to surrender to the police. But every time, she refused to let me. I owed my life to her for saving me. But saving me from what? The crime I didn't even commit? It was all her plan. Since she was young, she was involved in such things and always blamed others. But now, I guess she is the wrongdoer! I suffered all my life because of her deeds!" Ardhendu kept talking to himself and recalled every incident from the past. Instead of calling anybody and asking them anything he simply decided to confront Anurati about that 'night' and Mahatab.

"No more hide and seek, Anu! It's all over now, between you and me. Your distrust did hurt me!" Ardhendu didn't know it, but tears were rolling down from his eyes.

Within an hour, Ardhendu reached home. Anurati was in a very cheerful mood. She was excited for her due date, which was a week later. She immediately rushed to the kitchen, but walked slowly, and put the kettle on the stove. Ardhendu stared at her without saying anything. He didn't help her as he usually did. He kept wondering how she was so cool and happy. He was in so much pain, and she was so relaxed! She lied to him, and accused him of the crime he hadn't even committed. She is expected to do anything! She was no longer a trustworthy companion anymore. He raged within and went straight into the kitchen with his shoes on. Anurati sensed something was wrong with Ardhendu.

"What's the matter? You forgot to take off your shoes and you are inside the kitchen," she asked him politely.

"Is Mahatab Guru dead or alive?" Ardhendu asked, straight away. Anurati could not believe her ears. She moved back a few steps, as if she was falling backwards. "Is this what destiny wants? Now, when I was ready to disclose the truth to him, he has already found out about it from somewhere else!" she thought. She didn't dare to utter a single word. "Did I kill MG? Come on, Anu, for god's sake, speak up!" he shouted at the top of his voice, literally scaring her.

"Listen Aru…"

"Shut up! Just tell me. Was MG killed that night or not?" this time his voice was even louder.

"Aru please, you are scaring me and my baby." Anurati was shedding tears, which rolled down her cheeks and fell on her big belly.

"Don't try to fool me with your fake tears! Don't you dare to do that, you bitch," Ardhendu said, in a fit of rage. Anurati was awestruck. She stared at him with wide eyes. She was quiet. There were no more tears, there was no more shouting back at him. She could not believe her ears. Instantly, she pushed him hard and pulled out of his grasp, with which he was holding her tight. She started walking to the living room. But, before she could reach to sit, he caught hold of her shoulder and forced her to turn around.

"Ah! Aru, what's the matter with you? You are hurting me. God damn it! Can't you see that I am pregnant? Don't be my husband, but at least try to be a *human*!" Anurati shouted at him.

"I said shut up! What pregnancy you are talking about? I doubt whether this is my…" but before Ardhendu could complete his sentence Anurati pleaded, folding her hands. "Please Aru, don't question my fidelity. You won't be able to forgive yourself when you will know the truth. Don't be so rude. Think before you speak."

"Don't teach me how to speak. I know you are good at that. With that quality, you fool around with guys and you are so efficient that even live people don't regret being dead."

Ardhendu turned his back to Anurati. She sat on the couch, holding her tummy. She was scared that out of all these emotional exchanges, her waters would break. She took deep breaths to relax.

"Enough Aru, stop insulting me. It is unbearable. How can you question your fatherhood of our baby? I was about to tell you about Mahatab!" Anurati frowned at him.

"So he wasn't dead?" he gave her a stern look, and asked again.

"No he wasn't. But we..." Before she could say something Ardhendu clapped and criticized her saying, "Well played Anu, well played." He laughed out loud.

"I didn't play with you or your emotions. Believe me. I love you. Trust me. It was part of..." Anurati's voice faded and was almost muted.

"I am listening. Be loud, please." Ardhendu was standing with his back turned to her. Anurati was no longer speaking. She had fainted. "Thinking how to put to words and fool me again? Why the hell are you not speaking?" Ardhendu turned and was shocked to see Anurati lying with her head bent backwards, her mouth open, and her arms lying as if she were lifeless with her palms open upwards. "Anu, Anu?" he shouted.

Ardhendu came near her and sprinkled water on her face. No response. He could see she was breathing. He recalled her words about how he should to try being a human, at least. He tried lifting her legs to turn her around. He let her lie flat on her back. She was heavy. He was scared to touch her in this condition. He made a few calls and an ambulance was there in five minutes. The paramedics took charge of her and she was immediately transferred to a stretcher and pushed into the ambulance. Soon, doors were shut. He was asked by one of the paramedics to hurry and come inside, but he said he would follow them in his car and stayed back. Next, he dialled Lisa and called her to the Emergency Ward. She was elated to get the call as she thought Anurati was in labour and agreed to be there in the ward in no time. Hours passed. Ardhendu didn't follow the ambulance. He was still at home. He was all alone, sitting in dark. He didn't even switch on the lights. It was only some fifteen or twenty times that his phone blinked with no sound. Lisa was with Anurati and could not come back to check on Ardhendu as she was alone there. Her husband was busy with work and had not yet returned from office. Lisa had passed on a message, asking him to check with Ardhendu.

"Lisa, how is Anurati now? Did doctor say anything?" Anshuman asked, panting. He walked fast to the ICU from the parking lot, which was quite far. He found his wife sitting all alone.

"Nobody said anything," Lisa whispered in a tired voice.

"Has Ardhendu gone somewhere?"

"No idea where he is. I am all alone since he called me. Anu was brought to hospital in an ambulance, he didn't accompany her."

"I went to their house. It was dark, so I didn't knock. I came from outside. I think he is..." Without wasting time, Anshuman rushed out. He suspected something serious this time. This time, Anshuman parked his car and headed straight to Ardhendu's place. He banged on the door and pressed the doorbell. He heard noises from inside and calmed down realizing that Ardhendu was probably fine. In moments, the light inside was switched on and the door opened.

"Hi Anshuman!" said Ardhendu. His voice was huskier than ever, as if he had a sore throat.

"Hello, are you alright? You didn't come to the hospital? Your wife is alone in the ICU! Lisa is there since you called her!"

"Oh, that's great!"

"Great? What do you mean Mr. Mishra?" asked Anshuman puzzled.

"You said your wife is with my wife. So I said that was great."

"Okay, make it fast. We have to go to the hospital," Anshuman insisted.

"But I don't want to go there. Yes, you can take your wife from the hospital back home, your sweet home!" Ardhendu said, sounding hostile and cold.

"Are you drunk or something? Your wife is about to deliver your baby, and she is lying unconscious since this evening! Doctors are making all efforts to save both mother and baby! God forbid, if something serious happens, they may need your permission to save either one at the cost of the other! Do you understand what I am saying? Did you even hear what I was trying to tell you? Husband's signature!" shouted Anshuman.

"I don't want anyone. She betrayed me. Let the doctors do what they want. Let both of them…" he could not complete his sentence and choked with tears. "I loved her so much," Ardhendu whispered.

"Ardhendu, stop talking nonsense. She carried your baby. I am sorry I am interfering in your personal matters, but let me just tell you that whatever she has done, forgive her and forget it! You are going to be a father and she is your baby's mother! Do you understand what that means? Just imagine!" Anshuman said, trying to convince and console Ardhendu at the same time.

"You want me to forget what? Her affairs and her lies? She cheated on me!" said Ardhendu.

"Listen, I am just asking you to bring her back from the hospital. Let her get discharged from the ICU and then you have all the freedom to fight with her. You have that right but you cannot torture her like this! You will be in trouble if a social activist finds out about this. This is America. The punishments and fines are harsher than the faults!" Anshuman was literally struggling to take him to hospital.

"Hmm."

"Okay, let's not waste time. Come on! Get up, please! For your baby's sake, at least come with me!" Anshuman pulled him by his arms. The moment he heard the word baby, Ardhendu sank back. "Come on, forget everything. For my sake!" said Anshuman.

Ardhendu was still not convinced but for the sake of his friendship, he managed to go to the hospital where half Anurati's face was covered with an oxygen mask inside the ICU. There were wires, lights and machines blinking and beeping. The moment he saw Anurati, he could not understand how to react. Words jumbled about in his brain: wife, baby, liar, cheater. He caught hold of his head in his hands, and sat on the bench outside the ICU, next to Lisa. Lisa slid closer and caught hold of Ardhendu's hands and asked, "Are you alright? What happened between you and Anu? Please tell me. She was fine in the morning. And then all of a sudden..." Ardhendu cut in and said, "She is a cheater. She can explain it to you, Lisa."

Lisa was shocked at what she had just heard. For her, Anurati and Ardhendu were the most sensitive and committed couple! She left Ardhendu's hand and simply kneeled down in front of him. He was staring blankly at the floor, making every possible effort to stop shedding tears. "Look at me, *Jiju!* She can be a killer for your love, but I won't accept if you call her a cheater! She can never deceive you. I guarantee that. I won't believe you!"

"You are also part of it, isn't it Lisa?"

"Okay. So you want to know about Mahatab Guru?" Ardhendu was shocked and looked at Lisa, as if asking her how she knew that he was about to ask that."How right she was! She told me that you won't believe her if the fact came out inappropriately in front of you. She knows you so perfectly, *Jiju*. She told me that she will disclose the secret of Mahatab to you, but I don't know where she went wrong and what made you call her a deceiver? She should have hidden it from you all her life."

"Lisa, is this the way you talk with someone who..." before Anshuman could finish his sentence, Lisa stood up and pulled her husband and made him sit beside Ardhendu and said, "I am sorry I am rude, but frankly speaking, I don't know what there is between Mahatab and Anu. I can assure you she didn't cheat you. She told me this morning that there is something more than life and death."

"See, you also lied to me," Ardhendu said.

"Yes, I am sorry I lied to you, but Anu told me not to disclose anything on MG to you! But before assuming and judging everything, why don't we meet Mahatab who can clarify things? He is supposed to come to our place on Saturday. We all can sit together and discuss. What do you say *Jiju*? Please speak up. Don't remain silent."

"Ardhendu, I think you are over-reacting. This is just a misunderstanding. Sit, talk and clarify things with Anurati!" Anshuman said.

"I killed him some two years ago in front of Anurati. The doctor declared him dead. I saw that dead person. He was once my wife's lover! He stood in front of me, and he was talking to you, Lisa! Now, I am being blamed for being rude to that woman and cruel to that unborn child." Ardhendu slipped from his bench, kneeled down and sobbed. This time, Lisa and Anshuman could not console him. They were in shock to hear what Ardhendu had said. He took his time and stood up with the help of a nurse who passed them. He looked at both of them and again continued. “I killed a man. How does it sound? I had hundreds of sleepless nights because of this. But it was Anu whose love made me forget my past and with time, I was happy with what I was living with. However, I still don’t understand why she had hidden this from me for so long. Wait, I can sort out the things now. She was walking and chewing gum at the same time. I was a patient but he wasn’t.”

“Ardhendu, please stop creating your own stories. Once, she loved you. Admit that! Now it’s your turn! Trust Lisa at least once and let Anu be alright. As I said, make her sit and ask her whatever you feel like. She will definitely clear all your doubts. Don’t spoil your relationship. A single crack will shatter everything!” Ardhendu remained silent and listened patiently to what Anshuman was trying to feed into his blank brain. “Let me tell you one thing, Ardhendu. Be a man and pray to God that he saves both, your baby and your wife! It’s only the way you treated Anurati. She is lying there and fighting for life. I still remember how excited she was for her baby – for *your* baby! Just think, if something happens to her and your baby, can you forgive yourself?” Ardhendu remained silent. “Let’s call Mahatab now. Why to wait for Saturday? Let’s sort out things fast. The sooner the better. What do you say?”

Lisa was super excited at what her husband had just said. She desperately wanted Anurati and Ardhendu to be together, now and forever. Anurati was sensible at all times. She was sure that Anurati must not have done anything to ruin her love life. She was confident about her friend to this extent at least. All three of them got up to peep into the glass doors of the ICU to see Anurati, who was still ventilated with saline, falling into her system drop by drop. The baby bump under the sheets was going up and down. Anshuman asked the doctor about her condition, but he said that they were waiting for the patient to become conscious again, and that only then could they tell her whether to go ahead with the delivery or to discharge her. The doctor said that within twelve hours, if she did not get back her senses, she might sink to coma. These reports made them speechless. No one had the guts to call Mahatab. Ardhendu could not hold back his tears and again broke down. Lisa and Anshuman remained silent. There was a long pause.

CHAPTER TEN

Girish Park, Kolkata; September 2003

Anurati rushed to her college library, the day she just finished her Cognitive Behavioural Therapy (CBT) lecture. CBT was introduced as part of Physiotherapy courses as it showed tremendous benefits to patients with psychiatric disorders, medical problems as well as physiological problems. Anurati was disturbed with what she had learned. She related the textual facts with her past. Her thoughts shifted to Ardhendu's behaviour. The way his personality developed and changed. She analyzed these things and was worried. It was in a library where she thought she could sit alone for a while, away from her friends, and investigate what had gone wrong with Ardhendu. Now that she was away from him, the distance between the two had made her realize how much she was missing him. She had all the information she needed, about him. His first job in Bangalore, his new house in Bangalore – and much more, see learned from Aniket. She denied loving him, but her heart longed to meet him and have non-ending chats with him. She was happy that he was leading a normal life but was genuinely happy that he was still single. He didn't date anyone. So, he still loved him and is waiting for her!

"Whoa!" said a voice from behind Anurati.

"Who's that?" said Anurati in a loud voice.

"Please maintain silence," said the librarian peeping from his own spectacles which were on his nose. Anurati stood up and apologized in a whisper.

"MG. What do you want? Don't you see, I am busy," whispered Anurati at Mahatab.

"Oh my god! If you look into my eyes like this, I can't control my..."

"Shut up!" Anurati cut in and started piling up her notes and books.

"Let me check – love stories or..." Mahatab snatched a few books from her hand and started reading out the titles. "Cognitive Behaviour!" Anurati didn't feel like answering him. "Study books? I thought they were something else."

"Shut up and behave yourself," Anurati snatched back her book and went straight to the librarian to have the books issued. Mahatab walked out of the library and waited outside the main door. She saw him waiting and got irritated. But she had no choice. She tried avoiding him and walked as if in a hurry.

"Hello?" called Mahatab in a very loud voice.

"Please let me go, MG! I am genuinely busy. I have something to work on, something very important. I have to set something right! How shall I make you understand?" pleaded Anurati.

"You know, I love you. I have loved you since the first time I saw you!" said Mahatab very seriously, with his smiling face, no longer smiling. Anurati remained silent, and turned to the other side and was enraged with deep breaths.

"Hey, listen! You can't just ignore me!" This time, Mahatab grasped her upper arm and made her turn to him and was even louder. Students passing by stopped and looked at them. "Get to work!" Mahatab shouted. Mahatab Guru was a brilliant student, but cantankerous. He was the captain amongst the boys in the hostel. All he does was to study and fight. He used PT – Physical Treatment – as a solution for every problem.

He was a final year student, so the college authorities were relaxed, feeling that they would have to tolerate him for one more year only. He was influenced by his rich political family back at Rourkela. Without a word, Anurati tried pulling out of Mahatab's grasp, but it was strong.

"It's hurting me, MG!" He immediately removed his hold but didn't bother to apologize. Anurati stroked her right hand softly and gently over the red marks on her fair left upper arm.

"So?" said Mahatab.

"What do you want?" asked Anurati.

"I said, I love you!" Mahatab said.

"You know very well that I don't love you," sternly she said.

"Okay, then let me make something clear to you. I believe that *when someone loves somebody else, then that somebody else will definitely love that someone, someday.*" Mahatab said, pointing at Anurati while saying somebody, and his thumb towards himself while saying someone.

"Come and sit here!"

Anurati was tired after the lectures all day. And now, she had to deal with this stupid argument! She asked Mahatab to sit on the stairs outside the library. She was determined to end the one-sided affair once and for all. Now that she heard Mahatab say what he believed, she was even more serious.

"You know, if I start believing your *Theory of Love* then I must say I will fall in love with somebody else who loves me." Anurati tried making it simple.

"You don't have a boyfriend. I have known you from your school days!" Mahatab stared at Anurati. Anurati was about to say something but Mahatab stopped her by putting his finger on lips. "Wait. I see! I left school. After that, you had somebody?"

Mahatab did some calculations and nodded, counting on his fingers.

"Please don't try to create your own story. I don't have a boyfriend and my Orkut status is still single for your kind information Mr MG!" she shouted at top of her voice.

"Then why don't you accept me as your boyfriend? I have been after you for long! I am fond of you. You know my family. They know about you and your family too. Then what is it that is stopping you from accepting my love? I am good looking, educated and rich!

"Stop it please! There is somebody who loves me more than you do. There is somebody who cares for me more than I do. There is somebody who is suffering only because of me. There is somebody..." Anurati choked and could not utter a word more, and tears rolled down her face. It was the first time that Anurati felt a sharp pain in her heart at the thought of Ardhendu. She closed her eyes and saw Ardhendu: his eyes, lips and body. She could feel his breath and his touch. She could see those tears that had accumulated in his eyes when she rejected him, saying that she did not love him. Anurati was completely lost in thought when Mahatab shook her hard. "Anu, Anu... who is he?" Mahatab could not believe that he was roaring at her and was so desperate that if he came to know who it was, then he would thrash his head.

"Why? This is something personal," Anurati wiped her tears and immediately decided not to disclose about her rejection.

"Personal, huh? I will find it out," Mahatab walked away without even waiting for an answer from Anurati.

This time, she felt lucky that he was not interested in asking her for more details. She was also sure that Mahatab couldn't find a clue about what was between her and Ardhendu.

Nobody knew about them, their relationship nor his illness. Feelings were deep inside their hearts. Smiling to herself, she walked, holding her books, thinking all the way only about Ardhendu's illness and his treatment. She was sympathetic towards Ardhendu. Now that she was educated about what he was suffering, she decided to treat him as her first case.

Kolkata's Durga Puja is a very famous and popular festival. That year, Anurati's parents thought of celebrating it in Kolkata. During the coming vacations, Anurati planned to stay back in her hostel. All her hostel mates went home. She was happy and excited and was eagerly waiting for her family. They were expected a day prior to the festival and as it was a holiday for her, she decided to go to the railway station and surprise them. On the date of their arrival, Anurati checked her phone for the SMS which Aniket had sent and recalled that the compartment and seat numbers were B2, 26 and 27. She stood right in front of the signboard displaying the bogie numbers above her head. The train entered the station, and she was eager to meet her family. She was tensed about how they had managed in just two seats for such long hours. Aniket must have spent a lot of his time near the train door.

"Poor boy," said Anurati. She saw the train entering the platform. But her heartbeat was even louder than the noise around her. "Oh my god, why am I so restless? Why am I so nervous?" She touched her palm to her nose tip. It was like touching an ice-cube! She pressed her index and middle fingers to unclog her ears. She realized that this usually happened when she went for an examination. "But why now?" she spoke louder this time. No one was there to listen to her. She wasn't embarrassed. She was eagerly reading out the bogie numbers when she saw B the coaches approaching. She was expecting Aniket to stand at the door. What she saw, made her forget the numbers she was repeating for the last half-an-hour. It was Ardhendu! He waved at Anurati. But seeing him she was lost in her thoughts. "Is this why my heart was pounding so hard? Oh my god, he is so attractive! He loves me so dearly that his signals knocked my heart before we meet each other. This is true love. But why on earth am I not letting myself love him? He is so cute..." Anurati kept thinking and talking to herself when the bogie went some hundred meters from where she was standing. Aniket came calling her name, and only then did she realize that she was lost in her own world. "Hey Aniket, mamma and dad? What is happening?" Anurati was puzzled by seeing Ardhendu and Aniket.

"No no, it's only the both of us. They have seen this festival several times," said Aniket.

"You didn't say hello to each other," as usual he spoke again, non-stop.

"Hi," said Ardhendu.

"Hello, how are you?" She didn't want him to know how she felt for him. She asked without emotion, and didn't bother to hear what he said. This was first time she saw him after he had proposed to her. They hadn't even talked to each other since then, but they knew about each other very well. They were up-to-date, thanks to their point of contact, Aniket.

"Where is your luggage?" enquired Anurati.

"What? See!" Aniket turned around and showed her his backpack. He even made Ardhendu turn and showed his. "This is what we brought," he giggled. Soon, they left the crowded platform, hired a taxi and Ardhendu ordered the driver to take them to the lodge where he had made reservations for both of them. It was near her college.

"You are both going to drop me, right?" Anurati asked Aniket, but was eagerly waiting to accompany them.

"No why? Come with us. At night, we will drop you. Let's have lunch, and then we shall go and visit the *Puja Pandal!* Then, we can have dinner!"

"Wow, lovely idea. We will have fun together!" Anurati said. In a trice, forgot all her feelings and was enjoying every moment with both of them – one, her brother and one, a very special friend for whom she had special feelings but didn't know why. The whole afternoon and evening, there was not a moment of silence. Aniket didn't let any silence descend on them. He clicked many photos. They ate junk food at the stalls at the fair. Together, they played games of shooting balloons, hitting targets, throwing rings and winning nothing. Aniket asked her to take photos together with Ardhendu at many places. She realized that Ardhendu made every effort not to touch her. Anurati helped him without letting him know about his weakness. After a long day, they went to a Chinese Restaurant and sat together. Ardhendu excused himself and asked them to sit. Aniket was about to join him but Anurati pulled him and asked him to come with her.

"Oh Anu, don't pull me," shouted Aniket pretending as if she was dragging him somewhere forcefully.

"Now tell me…" asked Anurati.

"Tell you what?" Aniket stared into sister's big bright eyes.

"Come on, fast. You know what?"

"Some hint please…" Aniket teased her.

"I am serious. Speak or else I shall walk out from here," Anurati said.

"Is it? Okay! Bye! See you sister," said Aniket. Aniket took a fork and twisted it. He turned it in front of the light to check whether it was clean and pretended that she had left.

"Please, please… I beg you," requested Anurati.

"Ah! You are here? So not leaving? Bribe me with something then I can tell you what you are eager to hear!" Aniket said, winking at her.

"Whatever you want, I promise!" She rose from her seat pulled his left palm, and touched it as if making a promise and then sank back into her chair.

"You and Ardhendu Bhaiya are…" Aniket stopped in between and tapped his feet over Anurati's sandal. He thought he tapped her leg, but she was sitting barefoot.

"Yes me and…" before she could finish Ardhendu stood beside her, which made her silent.

"Did you order?" asked Ardhendu. He did all his talking with Aniket but meant every single word for her.

"No, we were waiting for you," said Aniket and looked at Anurati who was now furious. Anurati was completely out of her mind now. She thought Aniket knew about them. Ardhendu must have told him and asked him to convince me. If this is what he had decided, then it was not that easy. She would tell Aniket about his phobia. He was not normal. It is her life and she would decide whether to settle with him or with a more sensible person than him. She didn't even realize what she had for dinner and went straight to the hostel without interacting with them. The other girls were on vacation, so she only met with a few girls in the corridor. She walked all the way from the dimly lit corridor and entered her room. She was very disturbed. She had to talk to Aniket. She decided to call him the next morning. A rapidly humming sound, like a buzzing noise, woke Anurati up. She took her phone – it was ringing, and Aniket was calling. She looked at her table clock. It showed 5:00 am. She thought it was definitely something important, or else, Aniket wouldn't get up so early.

"Hello," answered Anurati, getting under her thin bed sheet and digging her head into the extra-soft pillow.

"Anu, Anu? Are you listening?" asked Aniket from the other side.

"Yes, speak," Anurati cleared her throat and spoke little more clearly.

"Soon you and Bhaiya will be engaged as per mamma and dad, so Congratulations!" Anurati was dumbstruck. "Everyone has agreed to the match! You were supposed to go home for the vacations and would have gotten engaged. But it was Bhaiya who said he wanted to ask you personally as you rejected him earlier. Anu, are you there?"

"Hmm."

"Anu, I don't know what you want in your life partner but I feel Bhaiya is a perfect match for you, a made for each other couple. He loves you a lot Anu." Anurati was speechless. She could not believe her ears. Yesterday, she thought Ardhendu was selfish and was using his tricks to be together. But after listening to Aniket, she marvelled at how great Ardhendu was. Generally, boys don't accept any girl's rejection and don't disclose it to anyone out of shame but he talked about it frankly with my parents and even came here only for me, my decision. "So Anu, what do you say? Are you happy with this proposal? Actually mamma asked me to check with you. Otherwise they will think of someone else. So tell me about your decision."

"Aniket, I need to talk to Ardhendu. So let's go to our college campus after finishing our breakfast."

"You won't tell me?" Aniket insisted.

"My dear brother, I myself don't know what I am supposed to say, okay? Bye, now," Anurati sweetly answered Aniket and disconnected the call. Anurati was lost in thought. “So he approached my family! How sweet of him! He loves me so much. I can feel that. What more than love can I want from life? I must call mamma and tell her that I too want to marry him. I love him!” But she thought about his illness. He was phobic and that too, he had haphephobia, the fear of touch. “He is scared to touch me. How will he manage with me as his wife?” She then thought of her parents, their emotions and feelings if she disclosed this to them. They wouldn’t let her marry him. She decided to treat him first before marrying. She would make all efforts and make him normal. Finally, she got out of bed, sat in her study chair and called her mother. She made a short call and said that she heard from Aniket and she was happy with what they were going to do. She could feel the excitement in her mamma’s voice. Now that she had committed to it, she was even more excited. She got ready swiftly. She took out her new green jeans and white top which her mamma had sent for the festival. The T-shirt had the words ‘Just for you’ written on it, but now Anurati wore it purposefully. She was so excited to meet Ardhendu that she even forgot to eat. She walked down a few hundred steps from her hostel to the lodge where both boys were staying. She only thought about Ardhendu the whole way. She reached the gate and was about to call Ardhendu, but she stopped. She again made a call and it was to Aniket. “What, you are at the gate? Come in then. Ours is room number 143. Come fast!” Aniket said. She again thought about the room number, it was 143! She and Lisa used this as their code for ‘I love you’ in school and chuckled with this thought. When a person is in love everything seems so romantic. Inside the room, both were ready and were eating *Luchis* for breakfast, with *channa dal.*

“Hi boys,” said Anurati, getting inside the room.

"Hello!" said Ardhendu. His voice was music to her ears; no more hoarse no more husky.

"Come sit here." Aniket asked her to sit on the only chair and asked her to eat if she wanted to. She looked around from one side to the other. She scrutinized the entire room. It was not a star hotel but was okay for bachelors. Looking at her sister, Aniket immediately said, "We are not going to settle here, it is booked only for two nights." The three of them laughed at what Aniket said.

"Did you have anything for breakfast?" Ardhendu asked Anurati. She was longing to hear something from Ardhendu.

"Okay, let me get mineral water bottles from outside," said Aniket and excused himself.

"Here is one," said Ardhendu throwing one of the bottles from the table.

"No, I forgot. I mean. I thought..." Anurati fumbled for her words. She was embarrassed. Her cheeks turned red and she started rubbing one foot over the other, which displayed her nicely painted toenails with green colour nail paint. She looked gorgeous. Ardhendu passed his plate to her and asked her to finish it up. He got up and went outside.

"Oh ho, you look ravishing! What's the matter, Anu?" Aniket looked straight into her eyes and raised his brows up and down.

"I called mamma and said yes," she said and shied away. "Are you happy?" she asked again.

"Of course. Thank you for doing that. I bet you won't regret your decision in the future!" They were silent as they heard footsteps of somebody coming from the corridor.

"Want to eat more?" entered Ardhendu with two more plates of breakfast.

"Hmm. I am hungrier now." Aniket winked at Anurati saying so.

After eating, they left for college. She found Aniket struggling to leave them alone, but Ardhendu never let him do that. She tried talking to him alone but she didn't get a chance to do that either. After walking a few steps, Anurati boldly stretched her hand and grasped his left palm. The grasp was quite firm and she felt that Ardhendu didn't make any effort to leave her hand. She was happy. After a few steps hand-in-hand, she felt sweat on her palm. Ardhendu's palm was clammy. She even felt the slight trembling of his hand and realized that Ardhendu was completely silent from the moment she had touched him. She found that he was breathing very fast. With all these symptoms, she didn't leave his hand. She wanted to know how extreme the case was. But she was happy in her heart that with all these symptoms and pain Ardhendu didn't take his hand from her. Both were still holding hands though Ardhendu was not comfortable. Anurati made every effort to make the touch comfortable till they reached her campus. Aniket was walking ahead of this couple, and was unaware of what was happening.

"The gate is locked Anu," he shouted from near the gate. Anurati left Ardhendu's hand, but before doing so she patted her left palm over his right hand as if she wanted to say, "Don't worry, everything will be fine." She gazed deeply into his eyes straight for the first time. She looked at him with all her love and affection she had for him, and smiled.

"See, come this side," Anurati asked them to get inside from the smaller gate beside the big locked one. The gatekeeper saw them and ran towards them. She showed her ID card and informed him that she would just show them the campus and introduced them. The gatekeeper didn't care, and let her in after looking at her ID card. Anurati was very cheerful. She described every division of her college and lastly came to the canteen which was closed. She saw the beetle shop beside it was open, and a few boys stood there with their bikes. She recognized them from far, but ignored them and continued with what she was doing. In the back of her mind, she was scared of Mahatab and his intentions. Without uttering a single word, she crossed them. "Hey Anu! Your brothers?" asked Mahatab.

"Hi, yes. No. But…" before Anurati could complete her sentence Mahatab cut in and introduced him.

"Do you remember me? I am Mahatab Guru. I was your junior, Ardhendu Mishra. You were the shy boy. All teachers gave examples in our class about you!" Mahatab raised his hand for a shake. Ardhendu remembered his face, his name but he was meeting him for the first time.

"Hello MG. You are here. Nice to meet you!" Ardhendu greeted him back.

"Final year dude!" Mahatab kept talking to Ardhendu, but stared at Anurati. He sensed that her eyes were pleading with him for not disclosing anything more than that.

"Great, you will be Dr. Mahatab, then!"

"Yeah, but what brought you here?"

"I just wanted them to see our campus," Anurati said.

"But I guess there is something more to this visit," said Mahatab.

"Yes, you are absolutely right. I am Aniket. Anurati's younger brother. The reason why we are here is Anu and Aru bhaiya are going to get married soon. You can congratulate them." Aniket laid everything bare in no time. There was pin drop silence.

"But MG is going to marry Anurati," said one of Mahatab's friends standing with a bike.

"What?" Aniket and Ardhendu said in chorus.

"Listen Ardhendu..." Anurati cut in Mahatab's words.

"Please stop it. It's my life. Let me decide what to do and what not!" Anurati was scared of Mahatab and his friends. She didn't want them to harm Aniket and Ardhendu. Mahatab raised his left hand and showed his palm to his friends, as if asking them to shut their mouths. He pointed a finger towards Anurati again, as if telling her to be quiet. Everybody stood still. He came close to Ardhendu, and stood right in front of him and stared him from top to toe.

"You are lucky that she loves you so much. I can see it in her eyes. She is madly in love with you. But I love her more than anything in my life. I can do anything to get her. I am helpless, because I can't force her to love me like she loves you. I can't forget her. She will always remain in my heart, preserved forever. Congratulations to you both!" Mahatab said. He went to his bike. His friends made efforts to stop him but he didn't listen. He just gave Anurati a stern look, as if saying thousands of unspoken words. Without any option, all his friends followed him with their bikes. With this, everything was out in the open. Ardhendu's and Anurati's love for each other, and their wedding. There was a long pause. Anurati thanked Aniket for spilling the beans and thanked God for sorting out the matter.

Over the rest of the day, they visited *Puja Pandals*, went to a multiplex, ate at restaurants and much more. But no one dared to talk about what had happened in the morning. The next morning, at 4:00 AM, they shall go back to their respective places. Ardhendu would then go back to his office, and Aniket would go back to school. Anurati was to stay back and attend lectures. While sleeping, she was very happy for the two days and felt blessed.

The meeting with Anurati and his relationship made Ardhendu think seriously about his illness. Back in Bangalore, he made an appointment with a psychiatrist to get treated for what he was feeling now, even with the mere thought of Anurati. He was scared. He knew he wasn't normal. But he was serious about his married life. Most importantly, he guessed that Anurati has sensed his trouble. He had to be alright if he was going to marry his Anu. He couldn't spoil her life by not touching her all his life! On his first visit, he elaborated incidents of his past. He recalled every detail of his life. He described all abuses in a modified version without disclosing Anurati's name and his hopelessness and helplessness for not being able to protect the victim. He expressed his entire feelings for Anurati. In the clinic, the doctor insisted that he should not hide any serious incidents. He asked him to carefully remember any incident that triggered his fear of touch. Ardhendu recalled whatever he could can and even described his symptoms that the doctor classified as mental, emotional and physical. The doctor heard him patiently and tried clarifying things. After an extensive diagnosis, the doctor confirmed that Ardhendu was suffering from a rare phobia called Haphephobia, the fear of touch. He tried explaining the disease to Ardhendu. Every case of Haphephobia was different because the core of the problem, that is, the patterns of thinking, the images, the communications involved were internally associated with being touched and are different for each person. Gradually, Ardhendu narrated his obsessive thoughts. He even elaborated his feelings of wanting rape his beloved, though he knew he would never do it. His anticipatory anxiety was like persistent worrying about upcoming events that involved being touched and those very common symptoms of dizziness, shaking, pounding heart, trembling, sweating and sometimes even numbness or tingling sensations. After a few hours of discussion, the session ended. He was relaxed. He was confident that his problem would be resolved soon, and that he could be a loving husband to Anurati. Together with the doctor he agreed to go with exposure therapy, and the doctor recommended him to a well-known therapist. He came out of the clinic and gazed at the visiting card and the pamphlets. "Exposure Therapy: a form of Cognitive Behavioural Therapy. It involves putting yourself into lot more stressful situations involving your particular phobia and overcoming your fear with new learning. The process will involve five steps: Evaluation, Feedback, Developing fear hierarchy, Exposure and lastly Building up increasingly difficult situations of fear after adaptation of earlier stages."

At night, Ardhendu emailed the therapist and requested an appointment. While doing this, he thought of informing Anurati about this, as she would understand the treatment better. But later, he was embarrassed about telling her. He wanted to eradicate the illness completely and then let her know.

In Kolkata, meanwhile, Anurati, was worried for every symptom that Ardhendu showed while he was with her. While she was young, she was not aware of touch, feelings, love and sex, but now, she understood every single word and the meaning of it. She thoroughly studied his signs and symptoms and came to a conclusion that he was a patient of haphephobia. She instantly opened her laptop and emailed the therapist Dr. Saxena who recently came for an open house seminar in her college and gave a long lecture on CBT. She attached her research notes and was excited to hear back from him. After doing this, she thought of one person who can work with her. He was Mahatab Guru. He was his senior and the final year student, who could take this case, as his final year project work. Most importantly, she could trust him to reveal her secret on

Ardhendu, and even he wouldn't deny her the chance of doing this to cure to love of her life.

Anurati met Mahatab and disclosed the past, although not entirely. She told him that she was quite sure of Ardhendu's illness and about the email she had already sent to Dr. Saxena. She was very professional while talking about all these things with Mahatab.

"Anurati, can I tell you one thing?" Mahatab asked.

"Yes, please," she stopped fiddling with the notes and looked straight into Mahatab's eyes.

"I love you," Mahatab replied.

"Oh it's so sweet of you. I love Aru and I want to marry Aru. Better luck next time, Guru," winked Anurati.

Now that everything was clear between them, they were good friends. They worked together in their practical classes. Anurati assisted him in his case studies and he shared his notes with her. Anurati was excited the day she received a reply from Dr. Saxena. She took a printout of the email and rushed to meet Mahatab. He said he would guide her via email, provided she furnished him with every detail. He insisted she carry on with exposure therapy.

"Hey, stop!" Mahatab was listening to Anurati very carefully when suddenly he interrupted.

"What's the matter?"

"Do you remember exposure therapy? A person has to undergo the same fear again and again before he is cured completely. I don't think this should be the treatment!" Mahatab made his point clear.

"But there won't be any harm. If we ask the patient to breathe properly and relax, no matter what the situation is, and moreover. Ardhendu, when exposed to touch, will be with me. What do you say?"

"Love is the medicine for every disease. When you are standing with him holding his hands, he can overcome this with exposure therapy!"

They knew the steps that were part of exposure therapy. They instantly made notes of all the levels of fear to develop the fear hierarchy. It was time to contact Ardhendu and begin his treatment. In Bangalore, as Ardhendu was under treatment, he was asked to start his exposure to touch. He insisted that he wanted to go to his fiancé on this. The doctor permitted it. Ardhendu was now in a dilemma. He wondered how he would tell Anurati that he would be visiting her very often? But luckily, he received a mail from Anurati, insisting that he come and meet her, alone. This worked as a blessing in disguise to him. The day came. After the official announcement of their wedding after the engagement, it was the first time that Anurati and Ardhendu were together, all alone. Ardhendu had planned to take her to watch a movie, to eat and then go to the park, so that he could spend time with Anurati. He could stroll around with her, holding hands, as directed by the doctor. The moment they started walking in the park, Ardhendu caught hold of Anurati's hand. She was scared, as she was supposed to do as per her notes. Ardhendu only thought of what the doctor had told him. He kept saying, "Talk, touch; talk, touch!" He started trembling. But now, Anurati diverted him with weird stories, making fun of almost everything, as she was good at that. He forgot about the physical touch he made with Anurati and was holding her hand tight. The evening passed by, smoothly.

"Anu, you are here? It's very late! You just cannot run from your hostel and come to this place," Ardhendu shouted, seeing Anurati in a netted nightgown which was small enough to cover her bottom and transparent enough to show every design she had on her bra.

"Shut up Aru! We are going to be husband and wife. So what is wrong if I sleep with you? I am not ashamed of sex! Come on!" Anurati pushed him and climbed on top of him in the single bed in his room in the lodge.

"Anu, are you mad? Get down!" Ardhendu tried moving Anurati aside. She was now leaning over him and trying to switch on the bedside lamp. She pressed her chest as hard as she could and switched on the lamp. Ardhendu could not imagine what he was seeing. Anurati was on him. He could see her half-naked body in a black netted gown in the bright yellow lights. Anurati took both his arms and tried pressing it against her body, but they were lifeless.

"Ah, disgusting!" she said, and left him.

"Ouch!" said Ardhendu and the lights blew on with his hands hitting the switch lying over the side table.

"Anu? Oh my god! Not again! What a dream!" He was breathing hard when he realized that it was a dream. He tried relaxing. The doctor had asked him to share every single thing with his fiancé. But he was scared to do so. He didn't utter a word and went back to sleep. Anurati was happy that he was at least trying to touch her. It was a good sign of improvement. Days passed and everybody was busy with their own thing. Anurati had a mail from Dr. Saxena and was tensed. She went to Mahatab and discussed it with him.

"Did Ardhendu speak about his dreams?" asked Mahatab.

"No, never!"

"Why don't you ask him what he feels for you? You are his girlfriend, right?"

"He will say he loves me."

"Duffer! I mean, what does he feel about your body? The female body!" Mahatab said.

"What do you mean?"

"See, Dr. Saxena had asked to clear the bad images in his brain. I think he wants to clear his fear of intimacy." Mahatab tried hard not to say anything objectionable.

"Now what are you saying?" Anurati was puzzled. She had never discussed such things with anyone, but Mahatab was bold enough to speak.

"Don't be embarrassed, Anu. It is part of the treatment and you are a good girl."

"I have an idea!" Mahatab stood up.

"Careful!" Anurati caught hold of the coffee mug which was about to tumble down.

"Call Ardhendu and have a one night stand with him," Mahatab looked seriously into Anurati's eyes and moved his brows up and down as he always did.

"Shut up!"

"Okay, call Ardhendu and try something intimate in his hotel room."

"What nonsense! You only suggest stupid ideas. Are you drunk or what? I can't do this. Never," Anurati shouted at Mahatab.

"Why? Do you have that fear of intimacy too, Ms. Anurati? Then let him suffer, and after marriage, you too suffer with him."

"Hmm."

"Then have a court marriage and then sleep! Bullshit!" Mahatab was irritated at the way Anurati's behaviour.

"I am sorry. I am really, really sorry! I didn't mean to hurt you!" Anurati caught hold of her ears with her hands and bit her lips, saying sorry.

"That's okay! Let me think of something else then."

"It's late. Let's go now. And yes, MG, one more thing. If at all I have to sleep with Ardhendu to cure him, I will even do that."

Now, for treatment, Ardhendu was again in Kolkata for two days. This time, he went straight to Anurati's hostel and surprised her. They had a nice time together. Anurati tried making him talk more. "Tell me, am I beautiful?" she asked him all of a sudden.

"Yes, so..." answered Ardhendu while sitting at a restaurant.

"How is my body?" She was bold this time. Ardhendu coughed and drank a glass full of water before he could answer. "Okay, tell me, do I look hot and sexy?"

"Shut up, Anu. Let us leave," Ardhendu paid the bill and pulled Anurati up, to take her out. "Now listen, you are very beautiful, sexy and your body is... your body is... I don't know. I have never seen it." Ardhendu sighed and whispered. All the compliments made Anurati blush. Ardhendu's treatment chart showed a lot of progress. He was troubled with obsessive thoughts. He tried controlling himself with some self-study but was unable to resolve any of it. Ardhendu bid Anurati goodbye. On his way to the airport when he got a message from Mahatab: "*I WILL SLEEP WITH YOUR ANURATI – SAVE HER VIRGINITY IF YOU CAN – YOU SICK IMPOTENT PSYCHO.*"

Ardhendu could not believe his eyes. He recalled that Anurati said MG had called her to his friend's house to deliver some notes. Ardhendu had to drop her at that place instead of hostel before leaving for the airport. "Driver, turn the car! I said, turn the car!" Ardhendu shouted at the driver. It was a busy street. Traffic was at its peak. He had left Anurati for almost half-an-hour. He started trembling, his heart pounded as if it was going to leave his chest. His mouth went dry. He tried relaxing. He had to save his love from that b*****d this time. "I am going to kill him this time! I never got a chance to do anything to anyone who has tried to touch her. But this time, I won't spare him!" Ardhendu spoke to himself.

"*Dada* – (Brother), everything alright?" asked the cab driver.

"Please just drive to where we dropped that girl, fast!" he said, and then dialled Anurati's number. The call went blank. He remembered she did that intentionally because she was with him.

Meanwhile, at Mahatab's friend's house, Anurati had entered.

"Hi Anu," Mahatab welcomed her.

"Hello. How are you now?"

"Come on, sit. Don't be scared. This is my friend's house. He is not here."

"You said you will give some notes!"

"No, Dr. Saxena will give it to you. He is on his way."

"Dr. Saxena?" Anurati asked, surprised.

"You didn't receive his mail? Oh! Busy with your Aru," teased Mahatab. Anurati peeped into the kitchen. She could see beer bottles and guessed that he was busy drinking. She was scared.

"Okay, let's go outside and wait for Dr. Saxena."

"Why? You are scared of me that I might..."

"No, no," Anurati cut in.

Beep! Beep! "*U B*****D – I AM GOING TO KILL YOU. I AM ON MY WAY BACK. DON'T DARE TO TOUCH MY ANU~*"

Instantly, Mahatab got up and went to the door. He closed it. Before Anurati could sense anything wrong, he hurriedly picked up the cushions and started walking towards the bedroom. He left only one cushion on the sofa. Then, he went to the kitchen and asked Anurati if she wanted a cup of tea, coffee or even if she can wanted beer or wine. He giggled aloud. Anurati was surprised to see the way Mahatab was behaving. He drank half a bottle of beer, and wiped his wet lips with the back of his palm and came towards Anurati. He pounced at her as if a lion had pounced at a deer. He caught hold of Anurati and gripped her hard. He dug his fingers into her navy blue cotton full-sleeved shirt and tore the sleeves off. Before she could react or shout, he put his handkerchief into her mouth. She could not spit the handkerchief out and he was heavy enough not to be pushed by a girl, or to be fought against. He was above her.

Thud!

"You b*****d!" The door opened with a bang and Ardhendu, roaring loud, hit him hard on his face. Mahatab pulled the only cushion and fell on ground. Ardhendu took the cushion from his hand and pressed it hard on his face till he could realize that he was not moving any longer. Seeing all this, Anurati was stunned.

"You are here!" she cried and clung to Ardhendu who hugged her very tightly this time.

"I am always with you, my sweetheart. You are mine. Don't worry. He cannot harm you anymore!" said Ardhendu, kicking Mahatab and caressing Anurati.

Knock! Knock!

Both Anurati and Ardhendu were lost in thought and were busy hugging and kissing each other that they didn't even realize the knock at the door.

"You are here, Mr Ardhendu? I am happy to see you with a girl, that too so close!" Dr. Saxena raised his hand for a shake.

"Dr. Saxena! You know him?" asked Anurati.

"Yes, my patient."

"My fiancé - Anurati," said Ardhendu.

"What happened to him? MG, MG? Get up," the doctor raised his arms and was worried.

"Doctor, please check his pulse. I will call the cops. They can arrest him. He was trying to molest her."

"But Mr. Ardhendu, I think you should leave now else you might be in trouble. He is no more. These are my students. I can handle it, but I can't save you."

"What are you saying? He is dead? I killed him!" Ardhendu sat beside Mahatab.

"No, you didn't kill him but you saved your love! That's it!" The doctor tried consoling his patient.

"But I killed a man. I should call the police and surrender."

"Forget about this. See. He drank and had a cardiac arrest. Relax. I will make the death report!"

"Go my love, my sweetheart. For my sake," Anurati kissed him and wanted him to be safe than in custody.

"Okay, then, bye."

As soon as Ardhendu left that place, Dr. Saxena handed over a white piece of paper that was folded, to Anurati. *It was a message: Sorry I tried to molest you, Anu, but it was a part of Ardhendu's treatment.*

"Oh my god, Sir this was all planned and now he died of treating Ardhendu, due to cardiac arrest?" Anurati could not hold back her tears.

"Stop it, Anurati! He is unconscious because of chloroform and he is alive. Check that pillow!" The doctor said, pointing at the cushion.

"What? Then why is he not getting up?"

"Mr Ardhendu pressed him really hard which made him suffer. But don't worry! He is not dead! I lied to Mr. Ardhendu."

Soon, they saw Mahatab moving his toes and palms. Anurati was relaxed. The moment Mahatab got up, Anurati hugged him tight and thanked him from the bottom of her heart. "I can proudly say that you love me! But better luck next time, my sweet buddy. I can only say that I behold my love and my life to you!" She cried and was about to tear the white paper when Mahatab took it from her and said, "This is the only proof of his innocence. Don't tear it."

They discussed the case and the doctor insisted that Anurati not disclose any of this now. She could disclose it only if she felt that it wouldn't trouble him anymore and he was completely alright! Anurati was surprised at the coincidence of choosing the same doctor and was happy that she and Ardhendu were compatible.

Destiny was moving the pawns, but it was love that was playing the lead role inside their souls.

THE BEGINNING

Edison, New Jersey; March 6, 2015

Beep! Beep!

Lisa heard her phone ring and opened her purse to take it out to check her message. After a long silence in front of the ICU, it was the only sound that echoed in the silent corridor. She opened her phone and checked the message. It was from Mahatab. She was stunned to see his name.

"I am at hospital, :"

Lisa was surprised to read it. Who had called him here? Did he really have links with Anurati? She replied, "Okay, then, ICU Department!" She didn't bother much about what had brought him here.

Beep! Beep!

"Who are you chatting with? Why don't you put your phone on silent mode?" asked Anshuman.

"I am sorry. I will do that!" Lisa said, and was surprised to read the second message from Mahatab.

"I have been admitted into the Emergency Ward. After three bottles of saline, I shall be discharged, so no trip to the ICU, Lisa! Sorry, next time."

"MG has been admitted into the Emergency Department," Lisa said out loud.

"MG?" asked Anshuman.

"MG?" asked Ardhendu.

"Yes, let's go," insisted Lisa.

"No, I don't want to meet him. You can go. I will stay here," said Ardhendu. Both, Lisa and Anshuman headed towards the Emergency Ward and searched for Mahatab Guru. Finally, they found him.

"Hi, what brought you here?" asked Lisa.

"Hello, it's a long story!"

"Make it short. Hello! I am Anshuman, Lisa's husband," Anshuman introduced himself to Mahatab. They met for the first time but they knew each other via Lisa.

"You both made it so fast. You were somewhere nearby?"

"Nearby? We were inside this hospital since the afternoon," Lisa sounded tired and sat in the chair in front of Mahatab.

"Why? Is everything alright?"

"Mr Guru, please don't move your arm!" The nurse interrupted and adjusted the saline needle, which was inserted into Mahatab's arms.

"Sorry!" apologized Mahatab. "You know, I ate a ready-to-eat meal, *Dal Makhani,* whose date was expired, from the Indian stores which you suggested, on your Oak Tree Road. My condition worsened enough – I was almost ready to go!" Mahatab pointed at the ceiling, saying so.

"If it was expired, why did you buy it?" asked Anshuman.

"Before eating, check the product's expiry dates!" said Lisa.

"They put new stickers on the old ones. On some packets, they even wipe it clean and leave the space blank!" Anshuman tried enhancing Mahatab's knowledge of the products of the Indian grocery stores.

"I checked the date when I had severe stomach ache. You are right! There was a sticker above the expired date from which I found that the product was really stale. See, now I am here with food poisoning. I will sue those cheats!"

Lisa instantly said, "We were here for Anurati. She is in the ICU."

Mahatab coughed, listening to what he heard. Anshuman tried giving him a glass of water but the nurse refused and instructed him against drinking it. She asked him not to talk much as his throats were dry.

"What happened to Anu? Has she delivered? How is she now? How is the baby? She had a girl, you said? She must be like her dad. Lucky guy!" Mahatab whispered all his questions. Lisa was about to tell him, but she felt nauseated, and sat back in her chair. It was a long day for her. She was exhausted. Anshuman asked her to relax as she was pregnant, which they had only found out in the evening, but didn't get a chance to share with anyone.

"Mahatab, you were killed by Ardhendu?" Anshuman asked.

"But it was..." But Mahatab was interrupted in between, when Anshuman said, "You had an affair with Anurati since your college days. It is for her that you are here in NJ!"

"Shut up! What nonsense? I love my wife and I didn't have any contact with Anurati since I left college. Now, I am here because of the conference! I contacted Lisa because her parents had insisted to my parents at Rourkela that I do that!" Mahatab was shouting at top of his voice.

"Sshhh, please don't make noise. You are disturbing other patients here!" scolded the nurse.

"I am sorry!" Mahatab apologized once more.

"Why the hell is Anurati in the ICU? Please, tell me!" pleaded Mahatab.

"Mahatab, Ardhendu blamed Anurati for deceiving him. He was so rude that Anurati collapsed and is lying unconscious since the evening with the baby still inside her!" Anshuman made it clear and simple.

"Oh my god, what are you saying? Blamed her for what? Okay, she had not disclosed the case study we performed two years' ago? Not yet? Why? She could have told him earlier. I have to talk to Ardhendu!" Mahatab was restless.

"Performed a case study on which subject? Not told about what?" asked Lisa.

"I don't know where to start and how to start," Mahatab said and closed his eyes. A tear rolled out from the corner of his eyes.

"MG, what's the matter?"

"Mahatab, should I call Ardhendu? He is also here," Anshuman asked Mahatab.

"She loved him so much. She was ready to do whatever she could to cure him. But what did he do? I am ashamed of even listening to this!" Mahatab said. Both Lisa and Anshuman silently listened to Mahatab, who was thoughtfully elaborating the past.

"Ardhendu killed me. But at that time, Anurati didn't even know what had actually happened. Only after Ardhendu left the place, did Dr. Saxena disclose our plan to her. She was grateful to what we did, but at the same time, he was guilty for lying to Ardhendu. She was asked by the doctor to disclose the truth when time came, but I think she didn't get a chance to do so."

"Sorry to interrupt you, Mahatab. May I know what the plan is?" Anshuman asked.

"Of course, you should know. I planned to treat Ardhendu for his haphephobia. The therapy used was exposure therapy and to eradicate his fear of touch completely, I planned to put

Anurati in danger and then made Ardhendu rescue her. Dr. Saxena helped me with this. I have the proof for it!" Mahatab said, and started browsing on his phone.

"Oh! Sir, are you alright? What's the matter?" a voice outside Mahatab's room asked.

"Yeah, I am fine," replied the man. Immediately, Anshuman rushed outside. Lisa and Anshuman recognized the voice. It was Ardhendu's voice! Anshuman pulled Ardhendu by his hand as he was reluctant to face Mahatab.

"Come on, man! Listen to what he is saying!" Anshuman asked Ardhendu to come inside.

"I heard everything and yes, you need not show any proof to justify Anurati's trust. That will be her insult! I am sorry. I know I am not…" Ardhendu choked before he could deliver his words.

"You should not have done this!"

"Please, Mahatab, forgive me. God will punish me. I am not in a state to handle such punishments!" said Ardhendu, holding Mahatab's palm.

"Ms Lisa? You are needed in the ICU. Please hurry up!" one of the nurses said.

"Oh my god, Anurati?" said Lisa. Anshuman immediately rushed, listening to the nurse. Ardhendu accompanied him too. Anshuman was so fast that he collided with the doctor who was coming out from the ICU door. "Ouch, I am sorry! Congratulations. The baby is fine. We had to operate and take her out and she is in the Neonatal Unit!" said the doctor.

"Oh, thank god!" Anshuman said, relaxed.

"Thank god for what? I killed her. I blamed her for nothing but now I will be blamed all my life for her death," Ardhendu sat on the hospital floor sobbing.

"Hey! Congratulations *daddy*. Baby is in Neonatal Unit for formalities and who is dead?"

"I lost Anu. She was selfless in doing all her duties but I didn't trust her!"

"What? Lost Anu? Why? Look! She is fine and her eyes are waiting for you and only you!" Anshuman pointed at Anurati, behind the glass doors where she had regained her senses, and was staring blankly up at the ceiling but tears still rolling down, non-stop.

"The doctor said sorry to you, I heard!"

"Oh! Actually I collided with her, so she said sorry. Now are you happy?"

Within an hour, Anurati was discharged from the ICU to a private ward, which Ardhendu had booked for her. She was brought there in a stretcher. The nurses moved her to her bed from the stretcher. The moment she entered the room, she saw Anshuman, Lisa and Mahatab in a wheel chair. She was puzzled, but still her eyes searched for her love. "Lisa, where is Aru?" softly asked Anurati. Ardhendu entered the room. He was behind Anurati's stretcher.

"I went to say sorry to my princess. In front of everyone, I am apologizing to you, my sweetheart!" Ardhendu kneeled beside her bed, holding her swollen palm.

"Please, Aru! I am sorry. I should have…" Before she could complete her sentence Mahatab interrupted and said, "Excuse me '*daddy and mommy*' no more 'sorry' time now only 'party' time!"

Everyone laughed out loud. Anurati and Ardhendu were delighted at hearing the words 'mommy' and 'daddy.' Anurati knew that Mahatab must have disclosed everything. She could sense the love in his eyes, still. She was his love. He couldn't see her in trouble, not even after so many years. She looked at Mahatab's eyes and could see his eyes filled with happiness. He winked at her. There was no more guilt, there were no more secrets. The only thing they had to do was to take care of the newborn.

"Here comes the baby!" The nurse brought the baby, wrapped in a pink sheet with only her round pink face visible. Her eyes were closed. With a tiny nose and rosy lips, she was really adorable. Ardhendu took the baby in his arms and kissed her on the forehead, saying, "My sweet little princess! I love you and your mamma too. You are my Anika – my strength. Anika Mishra!"